MW01135136

Copyright © 2015 Diane Lynn Collman

All Rights Reserved

ISBN-13: 978-1506181134

ISBN-10: 1506181139

Published by: Pelican Communications Group

OFF HER ROCKER

Diane Lynn Collman

For Charlie

...and for her, Frances

Prologue

I want to tell you a story about my paternal grandmother, who was a beautiful woman when she was young; genuinely, movie star-beautiful. She was slender with narrow hips and long limbs, yet voluptuous, blessed with shapely legs and a round, enviable bustline. Her dark brown hair fell past her shoulders and was thick and naturally wavy but perhaps most striking, she had the *lightest* grey eyes that smiled without her having to move her mouth - which was slightly crooked - and she smiled often. She had the most wonderful lyrical laugh, infectious to others, and she laughed easily. She carried herself with the grace of a ballerina, walked with a subtle sway in her step and was confident and carefree in a way you might expect the loveliest girl from a small town at the peak of her beauty and youthfulness to be. I am told as a little girl, when Grandma got to ride the train to Beatrice and back alone with her papa, she spoke to every passenger up and down the aisle. "Never met a stranger" was written in her baby book.

Her name was Harriet Della ("Hadley") Palmer and she grew up on a small dairy homestead, Fishback Farm, at the outskirts of the tiny farming community, Liberty, Nebraska. In the Spring of 1931 Hadley, the third child and second daughter of Ismay and Bertha Palmer, was eagerly anticipating graduation from Liberty High School and possibly a proposal of marriage from a young fellow she was crazy about, Arlington Hough. Three years her senior, Ari had been known and adored by Hadley for as long as she could remember - most of her life really - but only recently did she enjoy being courted by him in earnest and based on their enduring mutual fondness, she had every reason to believe in his sweetness and sincerity.

Hadley was the object of additional, abundant male admiration in her rural town and as such, more than a little female rivalry -- and she was aware of this. She was not much for studying yet she was a bright and capable pupil, certainly keen enough to realize this time in her life was a rare and fleeting season: Hadley had youth, beauty, freedom and opportunity and coming from a lack of family wealth or status, she could not afford to squander a moment of it.

According to my dad her home life was a little unorthodox. While she lived with both her parents and was sandwiched between two lively sisters, Hadley's mother had stopped talking to or giving her girls any warmth or affection sometime after their older brother Herbert - short, broad and too handsome for his own good; he was a ladies' man, not a gentleman - was accused of putting a girl from a neighboring farm in the family way, then skipped town to join the Navy. Mama, a heavyset woman with a wide face the very road map to melancholy, was now burdened by increasing deafness and the shame of Herbert's abandonment. She still cooked and cleaned and tended to the farm and livestock but moved about her chores slowly, solemnly, her only source of solace a bountiful vegetable garden. The girls did their best to stay out of her way... and out of her displeasure.

Papa, a dear man with a beautiful singing voice, (he belonged to a popular local barbershop quartet), had a kindness that shone through his eyes as well as his music. Unfortunately this good-natured father had in recent years been stricken with debilitating arthritis and though devoted to all his girls, he was essentially useless: in spite of his appealing tenor and even in the midst of her silence, Mama's sadness loomed loudest over their farm, casting a long and lonely shadow.

Lucille, the oldest sister and now a junior at Northwestern, was similarly lovely with her lavish curls, bright smile and dancing green eyes. But it was Florence Jean, or "Buddy", as everyone other than their mama called her, who garnered the most adoration, at least from Hadley. She made it clear her five-years-younger sister was the prettiest of all the Palmer girls. Round eyes, a jaunty pageboy and dimpled smile created an irresistible package, and she was perhaps the most talented. Bright and charming as could be, she loved to make up songs, arrange pageants and plays and demonstrated a budding gift for artistry, (perhaps living up to her nickname?). Hadley doted on her younger sibling and did her best to provide some of the nurturing and encouragement she knew Buddy deserved, but had been withheld, with Mama all but a phantom on their homestead.

Buddy reciprocated her sister's devotion and was Hadley's biggest admirer, following her affectionate, if increasingly mysterious, older sister everywhere Hadley allowed her. Not that there was very far to go in such a tiny community, and Hadley was stealthy, even secretive, that spring of '31. But Buddy, bless her heart, was still the most important person in Hadley's world - including her beau and admirers - and she would have done nearly anything for this darling baby sister.

PART ONE

"Life is what happens when you're busy making other plans" ~ Henry W. Guest

Chapter One

Hough Ranch was an impressive spread in 1931, beyond Liberty standards. It spanned one hundred forty acres and was punctuated by healthy and abundant oaks. Imposing stone walls attached to iron gates each monogrammed with the letter *H* announced the property and opened up to a long dirt road, lined on either side by tall elm trees, which led to its semi-circular drive. The main house was large and sturdy, white stucco, with a broad wrap around porch and the ranch itself boasted a beautiful herd of cattle and prize-winning livestock. The oversize barn had been bought - and then brought - from the St. Louis Exposition in 1897 and stabled the Hough's champion horses. They could easily afford the biggest and the best; always had done.

Hadley loved her visits there as a child accompanying papa and his quartet to various events and each July, the annual Liberty Independence celebration. Now as a young lady, to be invited as a guest to the Hough Sunday Dinner was truly something special. Ari, with his strong brow, teasing eyes and thick, wavy hair, (he had the most delicious widow's peak), was effortlessly cool and comfortable in his own skin; the phrase 'secure with himself' comes to mind. He was natural in his affection toward Hadley and held her unselfconsciously close -- and he held her often. What she loved most was the way Ari took her hand, simultaneously casually yet possessively. Being hand-in-hand with her sweet boy had become Hadley's favorite pastime.

Ari likewise was a carefree spirit and much-regarded for his standout talent running track, a keen ear for the cello, (there was talk he could become professional), and darkly handsome looks. Though born of privilege, Ari himself was a hard worker. In addition to being enrolled in a business program at Doane College in neighboring Crete he worked part-time at the State Bank of Liberty and painted automobiles on his rare days off. He had a wicked sense of humor, loved to roust not only Hadley but also his four younger siblings, was beheld on a pedestal by all the town and from everyone's estimation, so far very much living up to, perhaps even surpassing his potential and appeal. Ari was easy-going but sensitive, all the more so now that his father had been stricken with a grave disease, what is known today as pancreatic cancer.

That spring Rufus Hough did not have long to live and between the Crash of '29 and her husband's terminal illness, his shrewd, domineering wife was now at all times on high alert. Proud and haughty, Marion Hough had austere posture, a constant scowl the shape of an upside-down horseshoe, and wore her black hair, with its sharp exclamations of grey, in a severe bun. Her face was etched with deep lines and wrinkles, though more likely from her mirthless disposition and a proclivity toward chronic indigestion than true age and weathering. Their fortune seemed immune, but their standing in the Liberty community as its most prominent family would not be jeopardized if Mrs. Hough had anything to say about it! She monitored her children closely, especially Ari. Because of her husband's illness, her efforts to groom her eldest child to assume his father's various business ventures took on an added urgency.

In fact, she made it her mission to scrutinize Ari's demeanor and be vigilant of any distractions to her son and her plans for his future. That evening after supper, Marion decided to follow the young couple and ascertain for herself how serious their association had become. She was displeased, to say the least, by what she observed: a young man and woman far too comfortable with each other, too close and natural in their affection for this to be a passing dalliance. She would not risk a scandal.

It was early evening, the weather warm and mild. Everything was fresh and verdant and imbued with the sweet fragrance of newly-cut hay. A gentle breeze danced around Hadley's bare legs as she and Ari made their way to the big red barn with its steep pointed rooftop cupola, from which pigeons would often and noisily fly. He had been holding an arm -

alternating from left to right, then right to left - behind his back, but revealed it now, surprising his sweetheart with a bouquet of peonies, violets, tulips and lilac. She brought the flowers to her nose, inhaling their wonderful scent. Though Hadley was fond of them all, the peonies, tulips and lilac may very well have come from the front of his mother's house, but the violets were particularly delightful because they could only be found in the woods -- and that meant he had taken the time and trouble to pick them especially for her. He said the purple color reminded him of Hadley and her passion for life. He was always doing and saying nice things like that.

"Thank-you, Ari. These are so lovely. And my, I am full-to-bursting from your Mama's table!" Hadley exclaimed.

"Girl, you did so well!" Ari teased, and pointedly poked her in the side. "But we may need to watch this," he chided, poking further.

"...So now you don't like what you feel?" Hadley asked, mock-horrified.

Ari laughed. "Oh, no: if anything, there is becoming more of you to love. I cannot wait to get my hands all over you!"

"Ari! At least wait until we are out of sight of everyone," she warned, casting a furtive glance around the vast property. It seemed to Hadley they were always being watched and she was not sure if she was paranoid, or if it was because, between the many Hough family members and various servants and farm hands, there were simply too many people milling about the place for a young couple to have any real privacy.

They got to the stable, Ari pushed open the rough doors as Hadley set down the pleasing bouquet then fell into her beloved's arms, alone at last.

"God, you are beautiful!"

"Don't say that," Hadley admonished him.

"What, that you're beautiful? You KNOW you are!"

"Not that. Don't take the Lord's name in vain; you know it is a sin."

"Alright, alright. Don't get your panties in a bunch – I'd like to do that for you!" He was such a flirt.

"Ari, you have a one-track mind, you know that, don't you?"

"You love it, admit it. You KNOW you want me", He was so sure of himself, engulfing her in his arms and silencing her potentially snappy comeback with a warm, lingering kiss. He was as irresistible as Clark Gable, her favorite matinee idol.

Memories so dear become imprinted on one's heart and nearly sixty years later when Grandma confided her past to me, I felt like I was in that barn along with the two of them and my loins stirred as well; this is how real and present her recollections of first and ephemeral love seemed. I think time stood still for Grandma when she was Ari's girl. How happy and alive he made her feel!

The simple truth was Grandma felt fulfilled in Ari's arms, like she had found the male counterpart to her complete self, and she was natural and womanly in his presence. She became herself with Ari and returned his kisses easily, and in fact longed for more. Much more.

"Hey, Hads, I have something to show you -- something I think you might like". Ari coaxed her back through the barn doors and down a side path that led to a burgeoning structure. The new building was a smaller home, echoing the design of the main house. In-law quarters. It was also made of white stucco and beginning to take nice shape. It was charming, Hadley could tell already, and privately she dared hope she might reside there one day with her beautiful man-boy, her kindred spirit. Ari stopped to offer her a cigarette, a Lucky Strike, and lit it for her. They liked to smoke together.

"So Hads, I asked Earl and his fellows to set something I made for you into the I-Q's foundation... look down, inside there".

Hadley strained to see what he was referring to and at last she spotted it: a narrow board painted in red block letters with the words

'Ari loves Hadley'

"Well, what do you think? It is part of its foundation now and will be there for as long as the building stands".

Hadley could not speak. She was touched beyond words and held herself in check, lest he see how much this simple, plaintive gesture meant to her. After a time she wrapped her arms around Ari and pressed herself to him as close as she could, searing him with her warmth and allowing her body to say the words for her. They remained this way awhile, at some point easing themselves down onto a grassy spot close to the structure and taking in the fine evening. Back then, hay would be mowed and baled three times a year, as had recently occurred. The effect was a lovely aroma, so sweet and fresh, which pervaded the atmosphere; Hadley's favorite scent. Ari played with her hair, coaxing waves into curls, eventually entwining soft ringlets he had made into his fingers. It may not have been the fashion, but oh, how he loved her long hair!

Finally, from Hadley:

"...Why do you suppose when we are young we yearn to be older, get married, have our children and fulfill our destinies -- yet when people get old they seem to fantasize about being young and unencumbered and carefree again?"

Ari considered. Mindful of the sermon from earlier that day he speculated,

"I suppose because we are humans, our main sin is we are never truly satisfied."

"But that's not at all the way I feel when I am with you," whispered Hadley, unselfconscious now, adjusting herself so she could look him in the eyes. "Time stands still for me when we're together. I wish I could stay here with you and gaze upon this evening... forever". Stars awakened.

"Wouldn't that be nice?" he asked facetiously as he brushed an errant strand of hair from his sweetheart's face. "Sounds like Heaven to me..."

He squeezed her then and, after a bit, looked up at the sky, a feast of its own now with myriad stars shining over the young couple. They paused to take in all its splendor and lasted there a while. Finally, from Ari:

"It's getting late, Sweet Girl. I had better take you home before your mama starts to miss you".

Hadley scoffed. "Ha! Never! When the cows come home, that's when she'll miss me. But Buddy wanted me to read to her this evening, either Alice's Adventures in Wonderland or Miss Linley's Shakespeare". She had been neglecting Buddy lately and a pang of guilt assaulted her. Plus, she had missed the evening milking.

"Romeo and Juliet? Those star-crossed lovers? Well, let's hope for our sakes as much as Buddy's, your reading is not prophetic! We'll get you back now; we shall not keep little Buddy waiting!" Reluctantly, Ari pulled her up and lit another cigarette for them to share.

"Can we walk, Ari? It is the most amazing sky tonight".

He kissed Hadley gently on top of her head as an answer, brought her into the crook of his arm; his sleeve, like a youngster's, rolled up in a cuff to the elbow. Their fingers now entwined while her other hand beheld the pretty bouquet, they walked this way together with Ari singing softly in her ear. His was a whimsical melody made up as they strode along and she was amused then ultimately soothed by it. It occurred to Hadley this was the loveliest, most exquisite walk through moonlit fields and intermittent woods she had ever taken.

"Play your cello for me soon?"

"Always", he promised Hadley. Another kiss at the top of her head. And that is how he left her...

Back home, however, his mother wasn't having any of it. As soon as Ari returned from Fishback, Marion cornered her son.

"What, exactly, is going on between you and that Palmer girl?" she asked, eyes narrowed.

"You mean Hadley? What, EXACTLY, Mother, do you need to know?" he challenged, mimicking her tone. "I am of age and Hadley will be soon. You do realize she graduates in May?"

"Arlington! Do not condescend me; you know what it is I reference. And you must realize you have an obligation to this family, not to mention Hough Enterprises. Especially with Father terminally ill and so much at stake. You are certainly aware we all count on you -- and cannot afford for you to take a single misstep. You must be provident!"

"Be provident! What misstep?" he wondered. "WHAT are you referring to?"

"Do not be coy with me: you have become far too close with her, and I will not endorse your coupling."

Ari was suddenly weary. "With Hadley? Hadley Palmer is a phenomenal girl - top notch, actually - and I would be lucky to have her. What has she ever done to turn you so against her?"

"I agree she has a lovely disposition and she and her sisters are very attractive, but what of Herbert? He has been such a disgrace and thoroughly ruined any chances for poor Betty Jo Svoboda.

And you are surely aware that I have known her mother who was at one time quite beautiful herself since we were girls, and Ari, she is off-kilter! This sort of imbalance runs in families.

I fear Hadley will manifest these traits soon enough. I cannot have their disturbances taint our family. There is far too much to lose.

I will not have it, Ari!" She shouted.

Ari rubbed his eyes. "What are you telling me, Mother?"

He could hear noises coming from his parents' bedroom; Father was beginning to stir. Once strong and powerful, Rufus Hough was a shadow of the man he'd been just three months prior. Any sort of comfort eluded him entirely, the pain worse than anything he had ever known, emanating from his body in such a way he simply could not withstand it while awake, yet could never stay asleep either. Sadly, it would not be long now.

His coughs became more anguished. To Ari, they sounded unbearable and he felt sheepish for quarreling outside his father's bedroom when the ailing magnate was suffering so.

Marion, silent for a moment, waited to see if her husband needed her. Satisfied she could proceed uninterrupted, the matriarch pursued her course of argument:

"I know this will be difficult, even awkward for you, but you must break off your romantic ties with Hadley. If you care for her as you say, then you mustn't continue to mislead her".

"Have you lost YOUR mind, Mother? I think you must be crazy yourself! I LOVE Hadley. I have no intention of letting her go; in fact, I plan to ask her to marry me after she graduates, if she will have me!"

"This foolishness is precisely what I have been afraid of. I will not endorse it. In fact: I FORBID IT! I repeat myself, Arlington: if you truly care for this girl, as you profess, then you must let her go. Love sometimes calls for letting go the object of one's affection, and your commitment to your family requires your full attention now". Her voice was dangerously high and Rufus' coughs were louder as well, more fitful.

"I must go to Father, and you must consider my words a warning: Hadley Palmer is unwelcome back at Hough Ranch as your intended. You will tell her this in no uncertain terms - immediately - or I shall tell her myself!" She stared at her son, intractable.

Ari's head was spinning and he leaned against one of the dark mahogany walls to catch his balance. When he looked up, his mother was gone. Alone then in his room, he tossed and turned in his bed until it was a tangle of blankets and sheets as he replayed their argument, thinking - straining - for a solution or compromise, but it was useless. His mother, Ari knew better than anyone, was formidable. Hadley would be commencing Romeo and Juliet by now and she would go to sleep alongside her kid sister, cocooned in innocent bliss. But slumber for Ari remained elusive. Those same stars, once so bold and bright, seemed now to taunt him.

Chapter Two

The following morning dawned cool and overcast, thunder clouds threatened; all in all, Hadley's favorite kind of weather. Because of Papa's arthritis and Herbert's disappearance, it was up to her now to perform the difficult, often dirty task of delivering milk from their dairy and she drove a faded Model-T along bumpy, muddy roads for her effort. It was early yet when she finished her deliveries, parked Papa's old truck along the garage, pulled off his work gloves and started toward the house in search of breakfast. Her pony Missy and the dairy cows were in their pasture. Returned now from milking, the animals ignored her as they grazed.

The farmhouse was Victorian style - weary, white and rambling - with a waning wrap-around porch. A prolific vegetable garden was off to one side, though unsuccessful in its apparent effort to try and prop up the devolving homestead. Hadley looked forward to hot biscuits from her mama's kitchen and suddenly realized, she was famished. This is what love did to her and it is how Ari found her.

"Ari!" she looked up, surprised and delighted to see her beautiful man-boy. He was dressed in blue jeans and a flannel work shirt, haphazardly tucked into his pants as a young boy's might be.

His face appeared unshaven; his hair uncombed. No matter, perhaps they could share their breakfast now. The day, for a moment, felt bright.

"Hadley!" He called to her. "Let's go for a ride, shall we?"

She saw it then: Ari's 1930 Model-A Ford Roadster. A gift from his parents the year before, this automobile was very much his point of pride, so totally 'Ari': a vivid burnished orange two-seater with creamy top, spoke wheels, and best of all, a small toffee-colored rumble seat. Hadley felt high and mighty to ride in his car alongside her beau, but even more, she liked it when Ari put her in the rumble seat and toted his sweetheart around town as if he were her very own personal chauffeur!

Yet, despite the false cheer in his voice this daybreak Monday, Ari seemed ill at ease, not himself -- actually, not at all the fellow she had bade goodbye to last evening. Normally confident and self-assured, he acted nervous. Hadley had never seen this side of him and she became unsettled.

Ignoring the invitation of a ride she had to know, "Ari, what is it, what is bothering you?" His father, she guessed: it must be Rufus.

"Is it Mr. Hough? Has he taken a turn for the worse?" she peppered him.

Ari walked away from the homestead and away from Hadley. She rushed to catch up, pulling his sleeve to stop him. He would not look at her. Starving a moment ago, Hadley's stomach became tied in knots. She thought she might be sick. Something was clearly, terribly wrong.

Finally, from Ari:

"No, it is not Father. It is... Mother".

Hadley tugged again at his sleeve, harder now, forcing Ari to look at her.

A dreadful thought ran through her then: it must be Mrs. Hough. Might she likewise be unwell? She had to ask, "Is she under the weather also?"

"Mother?" He chortled. "No Hadley, Mother is as healthy as a horse". Ari was disgusted. But to Hadley he sounded disgusted with her and she had to press him.

"Have I displeased you, Ari? Did I do something offensive at Hough last evening... or afterward?" She thought of herself, in that bed she shared with Buddy, touching her body in its most private place and the pleasing, erotic sensation it gave her. Her cheeks burned.

Ari snorted. "Of course not. You were wonderful. Perfect... Always have been".

Nothing more. Ari's words, normally a compliment to be savored, hung in the air, along with the overcast clouds which now felt oppressive to her.

"Then what is wrong? Something isn't right with you this morning. With... **US**!" Her voice was climbing to near hysteria, but she could not contain it.

Ari likewise could not keep her waiting, her heart held hostage by his answer. He brought her to him and finally met her gaze. She saw in his eyes then how different he looked: older. Darker.

"Hadley, Dearest, Sweetest Hadley," he began, "Mother confronted me last night after I brought you home. Apparently she watched us in the barn. She is beyond displeased we have become so close".

Hadley considered. After a bit:

"We need to tone it down some perhaps?" she attempted.

"No, Hadley" he laughed ironically. "We cannot 'tone it down' when it comes to us. I am afraid I cannot be with you anymore... not ever".

His words - his mother's words - hung there still as the clouds. The lump in her stomach went to her throat, but Hadley had to pursue this.

Softly now: "Why, Harry?" ('Harry' was her pet name for him, a combination of Hadley and Ari together. She was of course the only one who called him this and it was his favorite).

"Hadley, I wish you wouldn't press me -- but naturally being you, you are always so direct. So if you must know... it... is... because of your family."

Hadley looked in the direction of the neighboring farm.

"You mean, because of Herbert and the Svoboda girl?" she gestured.

"Not just him getting her in trouble and then running off like a coward... it is... it is... your mama. Mother says she is afraid you will end up like her". He winced at his words, but soldiered on.

"With Father dying and so much on my shoulders, according to Mother, I cannot risk that".

"...And you cannot displease her", Hadley finished for him. (Who was the coward now?). She never used that word; she didn't have to. But she thought it! They both did. He looked wounded by her words, or possibly his predicament, she was not sure which. She hoped to wound him! For as long as she could remember, Ari had been her steadfast friend. Suddenly he'd become her mortal enemy.

"Oh my God!" she cried, bringing her hands to her face, as the weight and meaning of Ari's words sunk in: there would not, nor could there ever be, a future for the two of them. And in that moment she was not sure who she hated more:

Ari, his mother, or her own mama and her greasy, useless biscuits! Her body's impulse was to slump to its knees, to wail in protest and pound fists into Ari's chest and yet a part of Hadley recognized her worth and would not allow this. She had her pride.

And she had to go now, somehow pick up the shambles that in those few moments had gone from a beautiful life to one of ruins. Saving face was what she knew she must do. It was a matter of survival.

"Go, Ari! You are no longer my friend."

Ari did not move, did not look away, so Hadley said again,

"Go now, Ari. We are no longer friends. All of this foolishness between the two of us will be forgotten by tomorrow. That is a promise from me to you. I only feel relief that I never gave into you!

I need to change for school and collect my sister; I have my graduation exercises to consider and neither you, nor your wretched mother, can take away from that!"

She turned on her heel and walked as quickly as she could toward the old farmhouse, never once looking back. So Hadley did not see how Ari crumbled, how he was the one to slump to his knees and she did not hear his cries -- or how awful they sounded.

Chapter Three

She was truly running late and risked not only tardiness for herself, but also Buddy, who depended on Hadley for transportation. Her head felt like a pot ready to explode from so many thoughts threatening to boil over and her ears burned from the sting of Ari's accusations. Wasn't she ashamed, yet oddly synchronously relieved that she had never fully given into his advances? Then another horrifying thought occurred. She had become so indifferent to her studies, especially throughout springtime, she would really need to hustle to complete her coursework if she planned to graduate along with her classmates.

And then there was the matter of her acceptance to Northwestern. When Aunt Della, her mama's childless, widowed older sister had visited them last March, she'd made it clear she was willing to provide the same scholarship to Hadley as she had to Lucille if Hadley were interested, contingent upon demonstration by her niece of greater effort with her studies and a consent to care for Aunt Dee once she arrived in Chicago -- to assume the responsibilities of cooking for her and cleaning her apartment.

At the house, without a moment now to change, Hadley strapped up her text books, pulled a felt hat low on her head and shouted for Buddy to come, "Quickly, Sister!" Back in the Model-T with a worn lunch pail between the two of them, Hadley could feel quiet scrutiny coming from Buddy as she could feel her own heart breaking.

"Hi, Hadley," Sister said shyly. Silence. They jostled along, the old truck straining to keep up with Hadley's will to thrust it forward. Buddy - scrubbed, fed and eager for the day - tried again.

"Thank-you for reading to me last night, Sister. I love your stories. What must it have been like for Alice, I wonder? If only I could go down a magic rabbit hole -- I'd take you with me, of course, Hadley!" Still nothing.

"Sister... is something wrong?"

Nothing.

Another angle:

"Did you know Viola declared you are the tops of prettiness?"

Hadley softened.

"Thank-you, Buddy. And Thank Vi as well; that is really very kind of her. And you, Florence Jean, are scrumptious". This darling sister could always lift her spirits. She idled for a moment so that she might plant a kiss on the young girl's soft cheek. Buddy was a treasure, the glue that held their fractured family together.

Bump!

Jostle!

At last they arrived on Main Street; they might make it yet. They passed the Liberty barbershop, drug store, post office, three churches, three grocery stores and three filling stations. Hadley noticed Donna Dee's Beauty Shoppe, set between the dentist's office and First Congregational Church, and had an inspiration:

"Bud, I cannot give you a lift home from school today; I need to stop in at Donna Dee's. I am finally going to let her bob my hair -- even if it is 1931 and very nearly out of fashion."

"Oooh, Hadley, I think that will look swell on you!" Always her yes-man, this was Buddy. After a bit:

"Can I get my hair bobbed too?"

"Buddy, don't you think the page boy she gave you last time is satisfactory?"

"Maybe Marcelled then?" Buddy implored.

"Sister, you are only twelve years old, far too young to even consider marcelling your hair. Besides, I doubt Papa would buy you an iron. They come too dear".

They pulled up to Liberty High School, a two-story faded brick structure with arched doors and windows and a sharp wooden cupola at the peak of its roof that housed every grade. John

Hart, the high school janitor - not to mention Donna Dee's father - was ringing the old brass school bell just back of the building. Mr. Johnny would greet the students at the front door and help them off with their boots in the wintertime. Warm and wonderful, he was a favorite of all the children, and of Buddy in particular. She waved to her special friend as the sisters dashed into the building in opposite directions: Buddy, a flash and a pail rushing downstairs where the primary students were schooled, three grades to a room, and Hadley to join the upperclassmen on the second floor, taking steps two at a time. A bit of an afterthought, she rolled down her stockings just as the final bell rang. Covered legs or bare, however, prim Miss Tincher would be displeased.

She took a seat at a small vacant wooden desk and got out her Latin; Miss Tincher shot Hadley a look of utter reproach. When class was over, she ignored the other students filing out of the room and lingered to see if there might be a chance to sway the bespectacled lady.

"Miss Tincher, I apologize for being late again and am aware that I have missing assignments; however as you may know, I have taken over Herbert's route and it is stretching my time to threads. But I am serious about attending Northwestern in the fall and do not want to be excluded from walking through commencement exercises with the others".

"And you, Hadley, are stretching my patience to threads, along with your so-called time! Do you really think it is fair to your classmates, who have been responsible in regards to their attendance and assignments, for you to go unpenalized? Forget the charm. I know what has been robbing you of your focus, and it is not your duties at Fishback. I see you with the senior Hough boy, frequently, and if he truly cares for you, he will cease to be such a distraction!"

Hadley considered her words as Teacher continued.

"You are bright, Hadley, at times I daresay, promising. But you are also lazy and far too easily distracted.

Your aunt has made you a generous offer; you and your family are fortunate to have her support. Do not squander it or I fear you will endure a lifelong regret.

And do not try my charity further. I will give you until the end of the week to turn in your missing papers. Even your work is flawless, I shall mark down your assignments five percentage points apiece. This is my best and final concession.

Onward, Hadley. And go to college in the fall!"

Chapter Four

Hadley looked up from the beauty chair at Donna Dee's home salon, (a back bedroom had been converted into her household business; besides the beauty chair and opposing mirror, there was a shampoo bowl, a machine on a pole that held curlers at the top which resembled a floor lamp, and a maroon velvet davenport), at the reflection and wondered, who was this solemn, ladylike creature staring back at her? She turned her head from side to side and gave herself a slow appraisal. She decided she liked what she saw -- in fact, very much: the bob was fresh and light and accentuated her delicate features. Why had she waited so long to cut her hair? Ari came to mind and she felt a fresh stab of pain, but pushed it down as she had the others. Grief would have to wait.

Miss Donna, at the shiny gold register counting out her coins, seemed to delight in the-new-and-improved-Hadley and as she handed her change, along with a caramel for Buddy, paid her this compliment:

"The modern style suits you Hadley, if I do say so myself. I imagine Ari's going to love it". Another stab.

At that remark, Hadley couldn't get out of the home salon fast enough. Tears threatened. Back in the truck, she realized she needed petroleum. She would be hard-pressed to make it home to Fishback otherwise -- when it came to being low on petrol, she had already pushed her luck one too many times. She only ever had ten cents to spare. You couldn't get far in life these days on ten cents! She pulled into Liberty Filling Station and spotted Perry Wallace - a short, pleasant, sandy-haired fellow possibly ten years her senior - who claimed he was 'a wholesale distributor of petroleum oil' - yet who always seemed around and available to service her old truck. Perry brightened when he saw Hadley in the Model-T and gave her a wolf whistle, but she knew he didn't mean anything vulgar by it. Perry Wallace was harmless.

"Well-de-Hey-There, Hadley! What happened to your hair?" He whistled again, long and low, sounding his approval. Then he dropped the subject of hair for a moment to ask,

"The usual?" (Hadley had no idea Perry regularly added quite a bit more to the tank than her customary ten cents-worth).

"Yes, Thank-you, Perry, that will be all", but he was already cleaning insects off the windshield. Her plan, up to that moment, was to get home as quickly as possible, show off the new hairstyle to Buddy and bask in her sister's inevitable flattery, then buckle down on a mountain of overdue schoolwork. But now, hanging around the filling station and shooting the breeze with this affable man - and dodging his questions about when her papa was going to have 'Arli' restore the Model-T to its original black exterior - Hadley had her second inspiration of the very long Monday.

"Say, Perry, when do you get off? I'm feeling parched and have a notion to stop by Lou Lu's for a drink on my way home... are you game?" Lou Lu's was a well-known speakeasy on the opposite outskirts of Liberty, and no authority had so far challenged its existence in their small town or Prohibition, only the dubious gender of its owner and bartender, Lou Feck. Deep-voiced and whiskered - bearded, more like - he also wore odd, feminine-style shoes and had rather sizable breasts.

"I suppose I could be talked into a cool drink with a beautiful dame on my arm... but what would Arli have to say about this arrangement?'

"Oh, Ari is yesterday's news" she replied breezily. Her casual air belied hurt feelings - Perry could see this - but her attitude intrigued him: such a lovely young woman from a pretty poor family, who nonetheless carried herself with a lot of style and class. She obviously cared, deeply, about the senior Hough but she had the gumption and determination to carry on just the same. Perry had a fugacious thought: she'd make a good wife.

“You’re a good sport, Hadley, you know that, don’t you? Hey, do you happen to play pool? ” She slid over to make room for Perry to drive.

“Let’s see what this gal will do, shall we?”

And off they went. Hadley could tell this much: Perry Wallace knew how to make a girl feel special -- and he knew how to have a bit of fun.

Chapter Five

The atmosphere at Lou Lu's, while dim from cigarette smoke, was noisy and lively, particularly for a Monday evening; the crowd seemed in fine spirits. Springtime. Hadley was on her second beer before she looked down at her skirt and realized: she was still in her farm clothes! She had to laugh at herself and included Perry in the joke.

"You'd be stunning in a burlap sack, Hadley, and that's the truth. You really are the cat's meow, the bee's knees". She was warmed by his words, and no doubt the alcohol as well - especially on her empty stomach - as well as these cheery surroundings; she might make it through the hard day after all. Hadley knew her way around a speakeasy and she had her feckless older brother to thank for it: Herbert had found a way to buy beer and sell it on the black market and he always treated Hadley as though she were a lot older than her chronological age. She in turn had accepted that if she wanted to be in his company, (naturally, like any younger sister, she always did), then she must go along with what interested him: carousing, horseplay -- and plenty of booze!

A few games of pool and a while later - once again she'd missed the evening milking - Hadley was beginning to feel that this time she might have over-shot her limit: she had consumed as many as five bootleg beers and hadn't eaten anything since her meal at the Hough's the previous evening. She was dizzy from the thick air, wobbly from too much alcohol and doubting her ability to drive. Perry, still the good sport, announced he would carry her home in the Model-T, then jog back to the filling station for his automobile. But bouncing along the uneven roads unsettled her stomach further; Hadley Palmer was going to be sick. Perry sensed as much and pulled into Liberty Park so she might relieve herself outside the truck. He parked in haste, ran around to get Hadley's door and even held back her new hair-do as she purged the contents of poor judgment. He rubbed the small of her back and coaxed in a gentle voice,

"There's a girl, now. Let it all out".

In her drunkenness, Hadley confused his words and thought he meant to let it all out about Ari. To her further mortification, she began to cry.

"Ari has left me", she confided through tears, "and I am buckling under the strain of it all: the demands of my teachers, my acceptance at Northwestern, Herbert's route... and I neglect my younger sister so!" Now she was heaving deep, uncontrollable sobs. Perry held her there for as long as she needed and when she'd unfurled the last of it he settled her very gingerly into the

Model-T and oh-so-carefully navigated the remainder of the drive. His young companion was vulnerable and she was struggling, this much was clear. Something stirred in Perry then and he made a promise to himself: he'd watch over Hadley and do what he could to make life easier for her. He would not be the man who let her down.

Chapter Six

A new routine was thus established: Perry would arrive at Fishback before cockcrow, review the day's route with her papa, excusing Hadley from her duties and affording her some extra rest and the ability to get to school ahead of the last bell. When he returned the Model-T he had it filled with petroleum and brought hot coffee and sweet rolls from the Main Street Café. He encouraged Hadley in her studies, (Perry had begun his higher education at Cornell before his father passed away unexpectedly from an infected tooth and Perry was summoned home. His family was wealthy prior to his father's death but after his passing, former business partners defrauded Zachary Wallace's unassuming widow out of almost everything they had. Still, Perry managed to support his mother while he completed a business degree at the University of Nebraska), and urged her to eat more. She needed nourishment, he noticed - she'd become as lean as a flapper - so Perry treated Hadley to grilled cheese sandwiches and malteds at the local drugstore and on Sundays after church he escorted her to the Liberty Hotel for a family-style meal of fried chicken, mashed potatoes and homemade pie.

And he took a genuine interest in Buddy, teaching her to swim and fish at Mud Creek, a stream popular for its abundance of walleyes, wipers and catfish, and sitting rapt for her plays -- even proffering suggestions and improvements from the audience, his enthusiasm contagious. Buddy sorely needed the guidance and protection of an older brother figure and began to rely on Perry. In fact, she and Hadley both did.

Suddenly it was Graduation Day and Hadley's family gathered around in support of her after all: there was Papa, Lucille, returned now from college, Buddy, and even Mama in the audience, thanks to good ol' Aunt Dee, who was on hand as usual with her ready pocketbook and nurturing ways. Perry was likewise at the school gymnasium, (the school so proud of Mr. Johnny's gleaming butterscotch-colored floor), along with the other pleased-as-punch families and friends, but stayed in the background; his that day was a steady, if quiet, support. He seemed only to want the best for Hadley and never, to her relief, asked for more than she was able to return. *According to Grandma, when they finally kissed it wasn't earth-shattering - she couldn't recall the exact details - but it wasn't off-putting, either.* Young Hadley was by all appearances, and in large part because of Perry, slowly beginning to heal.

Mercifully, Rufus Hough chose to pass from this realm over the commencement weekend and Hadley and the Palmers were excused then with good reason from having to attend his wake.

During their graduation dinner at the Liberty Hotel Aunt Della announced that there would be a train trip to Lincoln the following day for all three of the sisters to shop for college items and a new wardrobe for Hadley, which had been merited in the end and was actually very necessary; when she'd looked inside her namesake's chiffarobe, it was threadbare. Aunt Dee had no idea how the girl managed to look so striking in such meager belongings.

Chapter Seven

'Summertime, and the living was easy' -- and yet terribly, insufferably hot. Hadley resumed her dairy duties, but tried to complete the route as near sunrise as she could. Miss Tincher paid a visit to Fishback one afternoon in early June, carting textbooks she had chosen from the public library she thought might be useful in helping prepare Hadley for the rigors of Northwestern. Lucille was home now to help with the farm work and household chores, supervise Buddy -- and Hadley hoped, exchange confidences, as only close-in-age sisters with a shared family history can. But she quickly learned it was a mistake bringing up the subject of Ari and her subsequent heartache. Not a dollop of sympathy nor an ounce of tolerance regarding the aborted romance was forthcoming Lucille. She had been a classmate of Ari's and very likely had designs on him herself. It felt to Hadley that her sister harbored some residual resentment toward her, as though, because she'd noticed him first and was older than Hadley, she was - naturally - more entitled to him. Lucille promoted Perry from the start however, and for her he was always a welcome presence at Fishback. As far as Ari and Hadley together, well -- she was nearly as unenthusiastic as Marion Hough!

… Once, while fishing with Perry at Mud Creek, Hadley had such an urge to talk about her former beau she could not suppress it, so she asked Perry why he had referred to him as 'Arli' that day back at the filling station. It was the first time since her debacle in the park that either one of them had brought up Ari, and her need that breezeless afternoon was undeniable. Perry told her how when Ari was a boy Mrs. Hough dressed him up like Little Lord Fauntleroy and forbade her son to play with the local farm children, thereby setting him a part from his would-be peers and no doubt frustrating this curious, energetic boy. Out of ear shot they teased the youth, and he spent more than a few years abiding their abuse and learning to ignore the disparaging nickname… After that, they did not speak of 'Arli', or Ari, again.

Chapter Eight

August now, less than a month until Hadley would depart for Chicago. Her days were shaped by milking cows and making deliveries, riding Missy, helping tend her mother's massive vegetable garden and checking off a considerable list of everything she needed to pack in her trunk. There was still some summertime amusement to help relieve the humidity and monotony: weekend movies at Liberty's lone theatre, The Comet, regular excursions to Mud Creek and Sunday night truck parties where a gang of her cronies would venture beyond the town's narrow borders, their final outing culminating in a trip to the County Fair.

Hadley and Buddy marked their birthdays, eighteen and thirteen respectively, two weeks a part. There was angel food cake and slow-churned vanilla ice cream for their shared celebration and as Buddy licked the last of the sweet treat from her fingers, Hadley appraised her kid sister and realized, a bit astonished, that Buddy was no longer a kid! She was filling out quite nicely -- evidently on her way to full possession of the older Palmer girls' similar enviable figures. Come to think of it, Hadley mused, Buddy's moods had been variable throughout the summer - at times stormy - not so much the sweet, sunny lamb she'd always known. The first of Buddy's monthlies began in August and so in a way, she needed Hadley more than ever. Mama remained staunchly impervious.

Chapter Nine

Exchanging her favorite hat for a freshman beanie, such was Hadley's less-than-auspicious entrée into life at Northwestern. Now immersed in college lectures and professorial demands, her hectic days at the university were balanced nicely by the company of her dear aunt and, for the first time in Hadley's life, a room of her own in Della's quaint apartment. She had just settled in for a second cup of coffee and some quiet study one September afternoon when she spotted an envelope, addressed to her, on Aunt Dee's kitchen table and fairly cried out with pleasure: inside was a letter from papa! She felt touched her father had made the effort - no doubt a painful feat with his knotted, swollen fingers - but when she tried to make out his arthritic scrawl, it was no more legible to her than chicken scratch, and she struggled to read his words -- let alone extrapolate any meaning from them. There was one phrase, however, that fairly jumped off the page at her:

'Your mama has gone and near-drowned herself in Mud Creek'

Stunned, Hadley sat at the small Formica table as she tried to divine the true interpretation of what he'd written: was he merely describing how Mama fixed to go swimming in the stream where her daughters and their friends had spent a fair amount of time in recreation that summer, and her attempt had been unsuccessful, or had she intentionally tried to end her life in an act of self-drowning? If it was the latter, then was Buddy, to her horror, aware of this spectacle and if so, what was the possible damage to her psyche, ('psyche' being a new word and concept for Hadley, thanks to her introductory psychology class, the one subject that had taken hold and really interested her)? She might have broached this incident with Della, but her aunt was at a neighbor's playing mah-jongg with a group of older ladies and she was loathe to interrupt her, let alone burden the poor woman with yet another of her family's travails. She couldn't risk telephoning home - every call went through 'Central', the town's operator - and it was a well-founded rumor that she liked to listen in on the good folks of Liberty's conversations, (the more salacious the better, *of course*).

Letter in hand, Hadley paced the apartment as she troubled over her dilemma: should she withdraw from school at once and go directly home to Buddy - SOMEONE had to take care of her, after all - or could she somehow get Buddy to her? She considered her resources and finally settled on the obvious: Perry Wallace. He had demonstrated he was as true a friend as she had ever known, quite possibly her best one. He had been writing her weekly since her departure -- indeed, was hoping to drive up to see Hadley and take her to the eagerly anticipated Nebraska Cornhusker versus Northwestern University football game.

Would he be willing to bring Buddy along with him, she wondered aloud? It was certainly worth an inquiry! Hadley knew her younger sister better than anyone, and this would give her a real chance to assess Buddy's well-being and determine if continuing life in the same household as their mama posed a genuine threat to her welfare. So back down Hadley sat, where she wrote to him at once.

Chapter Ten

It was settled then: Perry planned to drive to Chicago over the weekend of October 3rd with Buddy in tow and the three of them would attend the highly-awaited rival football game together. The early fall weather was crisp and clear and they certainly made for a jolly trio. To Hadley's great relief, Buddy appeared as vibrant and inquisitive as ever. Her pet sister seemed unscathed and so she said a silent prayer of gratitude.

After the fresh air and excitement of their day-long outing where Northwestern enjoyed a victory of 19-7, ("I suppose you would have rejoiced either side, Hadley Dear" he joked), Perry angled for some quiet time, just she and himself, and when the two of them were finally alone he pulled from his jacket pocket a beautiful hand-written card. Among other sentiments he expressed, this was her favorite:

... If you don't know it by now then you may never know: what is mine is yours and I what I do not have, I intend to get for you. Please, won't you be my wife?

Hadley was shocked to speechlessness: his proposal was the last thing she'd anticipated.

Here he was, this good and decent man, offering her his hand in marriage, and thus providing a lifeline to both she and Buddy from their shared destiny of gloom. She must not keep him waiting.

"Perry, this is so good of you, but so unexpected! Are you sure you want to take me on?"

Perry laughed, loudly, then grew serious for a moment:

"Harriet Della Palmer, I have never been more certain of anything in my life. You do a man proud". His words were plain-spoken, but Hadley knew he meant each one of them. She noticed then he had a nice smile. Before she could respond, Perry reached back into his jacket for another surprise: a long black velvet jewelry case. Inside it was a strand of ivory pearls.

Hadley gasped as she fingered the smooth, graduated gems. They were exquisite. She had never owned anything near as lovely and thought she might cry as Perry helped her fasten the delicate gold clasp around her neck.

And that was how it went for the couple: he would be the man for her, after all; she would become his wife.

Chapter Eleven

Hadley and Perry were married by a justice of peace the following Monday morning with Aunt Della, Buddy and Lucille all in attendance to their union, the bride dressed in a smart hat and one of the new suits Della had bought for her in Lincoln. Afterward the group enjoyed a gay and sumptuous Brunch at Chicago's Park Hotel. Perry read in the paper the weather was expected to remain unseasonably warm - at least throughout that week - so over their meal he announced what he would really like to do, provided Aunt Dee was agreeable to accompany Buddy by train back to Liberty, was take Hadley on a honeymoon trip north to Minnesota - 'God's Country' - he called it. Aunt Dee was entirely supportive of the idea, as was Buddy, who displayed a genuine excitement for her sister -- as much as for the promise of a fresh start for all of them.

So Hadley and her husband drove to Lake Burntside in northern Minnesota to honeymoon at the rustic Burntside Lodge, where a newly married couple could enjoy a swath of autumnal colors and some necessary privacy. The weather was indeed lovely and mild. The leaves were in various stages of change, their colors reflected magnificently on the lake. Perry taught his bride to fish quite expertly, they went canoeing to a nearby island he would one day buy and braved the frigid water for a swim - a skinny dip, actually - then feasted on mouth-watering walleye in the lodge's cozy dining room.

One evening over dessert their conversation segued onto influenza, and they discovered they shared a peculiar feat: the two had been stricken with the same treacherous flu of 1918 - Perry then fifteen years old, Hadley only five - and both had somehow managed to escape its morbid wrath. They set down their coffee cups and paused for a moment, smiling at each other across the table, enjoying this eerie mutual triumph they'd felt proud of in themselves and now each other: clearly they were both survivors.

Perry was a thoughtful new husband and alone in their simple honeymoon cabin, his attempts at lovemaking were tender, caring... grateful. He held her in his arms their final evening, snoring softly, and Hadley realized she had a sense of security, possibly for the first time in her life. And there was something else she felt: contentment.

Chapter Twelve

Mr. and Mrs. Perry Wallace returned to Liberty in mid-October and to his house on Bagby Lane. It was a plain white bungalow with simple wooden steps leading up to a front porch, similar to many small homes in many little towns all over the country at that time, and uniform with the other houses on its tiny street. Hadley found herself in her second unfamiliar kitchen in as many months and on another learning curve -- only instead of as a newly-minted student, now it was as newly-minted wife! There was so much to do to make his bachelor dwelling a home for the two of them, she didn't know quite where to start. But that morning when she opened the ice box and saw its contents near-empty, she had a notion. Alright then, she decided, I'll begin with a thorough trip to the grocery store.

There were three reliable, well-stocked food stores in Liberty back in that day, so Hadley went with the one most familiar to her and where her family had, for as long as she could remember, rented their frozen food locker: Dean's. It was a long building which had a screen door in front that creaked when it swung open, and where you could go after school and get a heaping ice cream cone for five cents. Today was Monday, one of the few days of the week where the bread man delivered. She was in the store between the bread display and a shelf of canned goods, scrutinizing her roll options, when Hadley spotted her papa near the back over by the Palmer's food locker where the family's frozen meats and poultry were stored. Simultaneously he saw his newly-married daughter, motioned her toward him and gave her a big congratulatory hug.

"So you're done with school, I take it, but it's probably for the best. Perry Wallace is a good man and you will learn to be a dependable wife for him", Papa assured his middle daughter. He reached into the storage locker and produced some fine-looking chicken and steaks and offered them to Hadley, along with this advice:

"Dot," (his shortened name, for 'daughter'), "Dot," he repeated, "you have always been a good girl to your mama and me and you will make a steady wife, but let me tell you something: there are probably only three things a man needs to feel successful in his household. Greet him at the door with a smile and a hug after his hard day's work; give him a kind word now and again to show your appreciation -- men aren't so tough as they'd have you believe; and have a hot meal ready and waiting for your hungry fellow.

And maybe one more thing, something I always appreciated: it doesn't hurt for you to laugh, heartily, at his jokes and pretend the stories he tells you haven't been heard by you already, at least a hundred times or more!"

Papa chuckled at himself as he returned the key to his locker and Hadley laughed along with him. His advice was straightforward and very reasonable, things she could certainly do for Perry. Perhaps she'd even dress in a crisp white uniform so her new husband could see how seriously she took her wifely duties! For the present though, she accepted the meat and poultry Papa propounded her, as well as his instructions to go home and cook a hot meal for her husband, and agreed to 'come out to Fishback for a visit and a ride on Missy once she'd gotten settled'.

As Hadley waited for Dean to write out her charge receipt, (it was then sent by a little can on a string up two stairs to the office to Edna the store clerk, who had a crush on Dean, while the bread man fancied Edna; a genuine small town love triangle, Hadley silently mused), she was on the verge of asking him to the newlywed luncheon Perry's mother was planning for them at Beatrice's historic Paddock Hotel, but then she thought of Mama and reconsidered the wisdom of extending such an invitation. Instead, Ismay told his daughter about a wedding that weekend which he and his quartet had been hired to entertain for in Wymore.

"It is one of the Hough's kin and I believe Widow Hough and her children will all be in attendance. Come to think of it, this may be their first time venturing out since Rufus' funeral". It hadn't occurred to her until then that the period of mourning is why she had never run into Ari or any of his siblings throughout that long, hot summer. Hearing the family name now wounded a little.

"Will Mama be going with you?" Hadley wondered, (along with the unspoken question: what REALLY happened down at the creek -- but, HOW to bring it up? Certainly not in Dean's!), though she was fairly certain she was already in full possession of the answer. Ismay told her 'no', so Hadley thought of Buddy and how her favorite sister would adore another change of scenery and the chance to be swept up in the romance and festivities of a proper wedding.

"Buddy, then?" she inquired. Papa considered for a moment, then said he didn't think it was a good idea. The ceremony and reception would go late into Friday evening, and he and the men from his quartet planned to stay in Wymore overnight in tight quarters, 'which probably wasn't an appropriate environment for a thirteen-year-old young lady'.

"Alright Papa, I'd better get these groceries home before they start to spoil. Thank-you ever so much for the meat and poultry. See you soon.

Tell Buddy 'Hey' for me, won't you please?"

"Okay, Sweetheart. I'll tell Buddy 'Hey' for you". Ismay tipped his hat and turned to go and then, almost as an afterthought, he turned back and began to serenade his middle daughter:

"Goodnight sweetheart,

All my prayers are for you,

Goodnight sweetheart,

I'll be watching o'er you

Tears and parting may make us forlorn

But with the dawn, a new day is born

Goodnight, sweetheart, goodnight"

It was a lover's song, one of Hadley's favorites, and as she exited the store, Papa's perfect tenor resonated in her ears. She thought to herself, surely no sweeter nor more intimate version had ever been rendered and it made her heart swell with tenderness for her dear father.

Chapter Thirteen

Walking back to the tiny house with her armload of groceries, Hadley could not get over how ideal the climate was, that feeling of early fall in the air here as well. October, she decided, would henceforth be her very favorite month. You had to live in Liberty, Nebraska to understand how few days of the year the words 'ideal' and 'climate' could be fit together in the same sentence! At home she organized her purchases, placing items in the ice box and straightening the cupboards. Glancing at the kitchen clock, Hadley realized she still had a fair amount of time before Perry was expected home, (turns out, he really was a wholesale distributor of petroleum oil!).

She ought to finish unpacking, tidy up the house and set about making curtains for the front room, but what she'd prefer to do was partake in more of this fine day - she was such an outdoors girl at heart - so Hadley ventured back downtown, this time headed to the drug store for a coveted shade of lipstick, rosy rapture was its name, and perhaps some new perfume. After her errands she chose to stroll home by way of Liberty Park, thinking she might sit for a spell in its gazebo when she saw by the bandstand, a white two-story structure with hexagonal cut-outs on the lower level and stairs up the center set, charmingly, right in the middle of Main Street, having a dipper of water from the pump near its side, and now coming toward her, a form as familiar to her as her own hand, and it took the breath from her, as it always had and forever would:

ARI!

No longer her man-boy - clearly all man now - he was more handsome and appealing than ever. His body leaner, jawline stronger and hair longer; grief evidently agreed with his countenance. Ari smoldered and Hadley trembled.

"Hadley!" he called out, thrilled and delighted to see her as well. He rushed to her side and swept her up in a hearty embrace. To be back in his arms, well -- it felt like being home.

"It is SO GOOD to see you again!" he exclaimed, then held her away from him so he might have a better look at her.

"My God! You are more beautiful, more radiant than ever... but what happened to your hair?"

Hadley could feel her heart pounding against her chest, so loudly she feared he could hear it as well. Her stomach rumbled... her hands grew clammy... her cheeks flushed... it was as though her senses were being aroused, one by one: Hadley Palmer Wallace was coming back to life.

Chapter Fourteen

She brought her hands to her hair and finally managed,

"I -- I bobbed my hair, but that was ages ago, really. It's nearly grown out by now, I'm fairly sure". Hadley knew she was rambling, doubtless sounding like an idiot.

But Ari was no longer looking at the strange new hair-do; something else had caught his eye: a shiny gold wedding band Hadley wore on her left-hand ring finger.

"What the Hell?" he asked, snatching her hand a bit roughly, so he could get a closer look at what he thought he'd just seen.

"What the FUCK?"

Hadley was stung by his language - words she'd heard Herbert use, never Ari - and she could feel his confusion and an anger towards her, of all people, rising.

"Jesus Christ, Hadley, you sure didn't waste any time! Who's the lucky guy?" He looked so wounded.

Her face grew hot.

"I -- I -- it's Perry Wallace. We eloped not quite two weeks ago. We've only just returned from our honey—"

"Fucking Perry Wallace?" Ari interrupted her. "That guy is WAY too old for you. He took advantage!" He was outraged now.

Hadley was not used to anger in him, especially toward her, while she herself was experiencing a jumble of so many strong and conflicting emotions: WHAT in the world had she just done, marrying this older man she didn't really know, and so hastily? HOW could she have EVER thought she was over, could even GET OVER, Ari? And a pure fury toward Ari for acting as though she were his possession, when he had dropped her so totally -- and without any sort of protest from him against his hateful mother. He had a lot of nerve accusing her this way, as though she were the villain in this whole sordid mess.

"Do you love him? Hads? Do you actually love this guy?" Ari bombarded her.

"I - I thought I... He has been so good to me - and to Buddy".

"BUDDY?! Hadley, you don't go off and marry a fellow 'cause he's been good to your kid sister!" he cried. "WHY didn't you wait for me?!"

"Ari, you gave me no hope, no reason whatsoever, to believe you were ever coming back. In fact, you thoroughly humiliated me and callously broke my heart. How DARE you treat me now as if I were the one in the wrong?"

Ari recoiled at once from this undeniable, stinging accusation: they both new full well that he had never taken up for her, for 'his girl'. And he knew something else: his mother had told him all about Bertha Palmer and her disastrous escapade in Mud Creek, so he softened immediately as he was chastened that this girl before him was doing the best she could for herself, and certainly by Buddy. He had to admit he admired her: Hadley was the stronger of the two. (WHY hadn't he stood up to Marion?) Look what it cost him!

Coming to his senses, Ari raked his hair as he surveyed the area, noticing some old men sitting in the shade playing cards as well as a cluster of "blue hairs", (ladies who frequented Donna Dee's for a bluing tint to avoid their white hair turning yellow), visiting, and realized they could not risk continuing this very personal conversation in public and he was desperate to talk to her, to pick her brain a bit further. If her marriage was so recent, perhaps it could be undone just as swiftly.

"Hadley, this is no place to have privacy for the talk we need to have. We must set things right! If you have any love left for me, even a little, we deserve to work this out -- but out of sight of nosey busybodies and town gossips. Please, tell me you'll agree to meet me somewhere private? We've got to settle things. Tell me I still have a chance with you!"

He took her elbow and steered her back toward the water pump and by the shelter of the windmill and some overgrown rose bushes.

"When can I see you, Hadley? There is nothing I won't do to get you back!"

"Ari", she soothed, likewise realizing she was risking a spectacle -- but then her raging heart betrayed her.

"I do love you, Ari, more than ever". There. "I'm afraid I have made such a mess of things!" It was out. Her heart wanted what it wanted, and yet for possibly the first time in her life Hadley feared she had gotten herself - not to mention innocent others - into something she couldn't undo.

"Say it again, Hads. Say, 'I love you, Harry' " he beseeched her.

"I love you... Harry. Truthfully speaking, I adore you. I never stopped... I never could". It was out now, and there was no conceivable way she could take her feelings back.

"My cousin Howard is getting married in Wymore on Friday evening. Is there any chance you can get away and meet me at the ranch?" Ari concocted, heading them away from the windmill -- and away from watchful old biddies.

"What about your mother? Aren't you expected to attend the reception as well?" she challenged.

"No. Mother thinks I am in Crete, overwhelmed with finishing up my business degree at Doane before Christmas. She has not pressed me too terribly lately. She would never suspect I've come back to the ranch instead. And the rest of the family is going - it is their first time out from mourning - so I am sure the household staff will be scarce throughout the weekend.

What do you suppose, Hads? Could you make up some excuse and meet me there Friday night?"

The couple walked in the direction of the grain elevator as Hadley considered.

"What shall I tell Perry?" she asked. She thought of her previous conversation with papa and the image of a lonely Buddy stuck at Fishback by herself, yet again.

"That I need to go over to Fishback and spend the night with Buddy?" she mused. "Is that believable?"

"Can you convince him he'll be fine without you for one night -- but Buddy won't? Can you say that?" Ari pressed her.

Hadley thought for a moment, pushing away images of Perry's kind face, his goodness... and

Buddy's isolation: all that mattered at this moment was being back in Ari's arms again, where she belonged. She would deny herself no longer.

"I can do this, Ari: I can find a way to meet you at Hough on Friday evening. Six o'clock?"

"Six o'clock, then. I will be there waiting for you outside the front gates of the ranch, and this time I will fight for you, Hadley! I will not disappoint you or hurt you again.

... I'd die first".

"Oh Ari, me too!" she cried. "I'd rather die than have to be without you ever again!"

Chapter Fifteen

It was only Tuesday and already Hadley was a wreck. How would she last the next few days without her man? And how could she maintain a facade of happiness and normalcy around Perry and about town? The minutes seemed to drag by, so Hadley tried to occupy the endless hours by arranging their new household -- even though it felt like such a lie on her part, and she hated herself for it. Making matters worse, Perry cleared all his hunting and fishing equipment and tools from the spare room, insisting they set it up as a second bedroom for Buddy, 'so whenever the young teen had the need or desire to stay there, she would feel welcome'. Hadley went about making gingham curtains in her sister's favorite color, knowing all the while her pet sister would never set foot in there - let alone spend the night - if she and Ari had their way. Oh, she must have the blackest heart, and not a single person she could talk to about any of this! Her only consolation was that she would soon be reunited with Ari and when they were finally together, everyone would see how right they were, the ultimate fit. How could a love like theirs be wrong?

Wednesday nights were met with a bit of fanfare in Liberty, particularly during mild weather. Stores and businesses stayed open throughout the evening and after farmers' wives had sold their eggs and cream, and thus had spending money with which to buy their family's weekly supply of food and household goods, there was usually a little left over for a slice of pie and some coffee at the Liberty Café. Children and teenagers roamed the streets while the menfolk slipped over to Lou Lu's for a drink or two.

The Comet held free shows outside the theatre on Wednesdays where there would be planks set up on which its patrons could sit; this particular evening the marquis announced they were playing Vina Delmar's "Bad Girl". The film had been released back on August 13th of that year, but had just now made its way to the tiny farm town. Warm weather Wednesday nights really were something to look forward to in the small farming community and most everyone turned out for them. This movie however was far too close to Hadley as it paralleled her discomforting situation; had it been anyone else's predicament, she would have found the irony in the title of the film wickedly funny and enjoyed a mean and hearty giggle with her girlfriends -- if only it weren't all so pathetically spot-on with her private torment.

And after seeing Ari, this 'bad girl' did not think she had it in her to maintain the charade of happy new bride - not to mention the inevitable display of showing her wedding ring to her pals - so she begged off with a headache and she and

Perry remained at home. Over supper he must have yet had commerce on his mind because he brought up that a small new store that had been established out near Fishback.

"Were you aware of this, Hadley?" He asked his distracted wife.

"I don't know the owners, but it will be more convenient for Ismay - and certainly Buddy - though, with your approval, I'd like to start teaching her to drive the Model-T". He could tell she was preoccupied.

"Hadley. Didn't you begin driving before you were even twelve years old? Why, Buddy's practically over-the-hill compared to you!"

...This snapped her back to reality and gave her the lead-in to her scheme, so Hadley broached the subject of spending Friday night at Fishback with her sister - the shame of her deception so bright on her cheeks, she was certain they were scarlet - and her plans with Ari transparent. But Perry actually encouraged this and figured he might stay up in Beatrice with his mother, where they were putting the finishing touches on the celebratory newlywed luncheon, "...unless you need me to drive you over in the Chevy?" he offered. Oh, he was too dear for her! Hadley knew then that she did not deserve him and wished she could dissolve into her chair. She was becoming viler by the hour, the wait until Friday now an interminable Hell for her.

Thursday afternoon the Wallace's crank telephone trilled with a call from Central, trying to connect Buddy on the line.

"Hadley!" she cried when she heard her sister's voice on the other end. "How was your honeymoon trip to the woods of northern Minnesota?"

"Oh Buddy, Dear, it's so nice to hear your voice", she answered weakly. "Our trip was most satisfactory and Perry is correct: Minnesota must be God's Country". What a wicked girl she was!

"Did you catch many fish?" Buddy wondered.

"We did, Sister, and we went swimming and canoeing to an island. I brought you back a postcard of Lake Burntside, and some moccasins".

"Thank-you, Hadley. I cannot wait to see them! May I come over?" Buddy implored. "Papa is singing with his Quartet at a wedding up in Wymore Friday night... maybe I could stay with you -- and my new brother-in-law!" She laughed at the strange way this sounded to say out loud for the first time.

Hadley laughed too, if a bit nervously. "I am afraid we're not set up to have you just yet, Bud... but I'll tell you what: if Perry doesn't need me and I can get a lift to Fishback, I will drop in for a visit Friday evening; how would that be?"

She had never before, as far as she could recall, lied to her younger sister and Hadley's conscience flared up at her: could she actually go through with this mendacity? Love was turning her into a horrible, monstrous person. She did not recognize who she had become in three short days!

"I would love that, Sister. You could bring my presents, and maybe we could pull some taffy?"

"If Perry doesn't need me, I'll bring your things. If he doesn't need me, we can pull taffy".

Hadley didn't say goodbye. A lie to Buddy was a sin. She had to go now.

Chapter Sixteen

Friday. At last. But a cold spell had settled into Liberty overnight and the tiny town awakened covered by a blanket of frost. Hadley peered through the curtain of her bedroom window and wondered, was this a sign? Should she not go through with her rendezvous with Ari after all? She wrapped a thick robe around herself and began to make up their bed. She could still feel the warmth from hers and Perry's bodies in the blankets and sheets and the sensation recalled for Hadley their previous evening when he had reached for his wife in the middle of the night and she'd denied him, claiming it was her time of month. Perry didn't seem to mind, had offered to cuddle her instead and ended up rubbing the small of her back -- just as he had their first evening together in the park where she'd made such a spectacle of herself.

Was she SURE she wanted to do this? Because when she walked out that door, she would not be coming back to him and their fragile new life here, at least not the same as she was now; in fact, Hadley felt like a stranger to herself already. She paced the tiny house and wished, ephemerally, that she had a dog she could pet and be comforted by; she was becoming overwrought. In the kitchen she couldn't eat a thing - of course - and when she tried to fix herself a cup of coffee, her hands shook so badly she nearly broke the saucer. Then, while she succeeded in bringing the cup to her lips, she accidentally scalded her tongue.

She turned on the radio in an attempt to soothe her frayed nerves hoping to perhaps hear something by Kate Smith, but instead she found "I Surrender, Dear" playing on one station and "Dancing in the Dark" on another, both of which sounded terribly vexing to her - not to mention acridly prophetic - and she quickly switched it back off. Then she tried to read, but it was of no use, so she finally settled on a hot bath, one as steamy as she could tolerate, and said a prayer of thanks to both God and Perry for indoor plumbing. Images of Buddy traipsing to the outhouse in the frigid weather, frost on her breath, flashed before her eyes and Hadley had to force them away. She willed herself not to think of her younger sister again - at least for this day - and it took all the effort she could summon -- THAT was how foreign a sensation it was for her not to want to consider Buddy. Instead, as she sat inside the cold, hard tub with her head resting against its cold, hard lip until the water was cool as well, she noticed, likely for the first time, the faded wallpaper with its winsome pattern of roses and bows that covered their bathroom and for some reason, it endeared her to Perry -- even made her feel a bit protective of her new husband.

She took more time and care with her grooming than she ever had, painstakingly marcelling her hair, as was still the fashion, applying both rouge and the rosy shade of lipstick to her face to the point of vanity, though she had never before been vain. She dabbed the new drugstore perfume behind both ears, at her wrists... and a dot or two along her cleavage.

Then she scrutinized her wardrobe, at last selecting the finest suit Aunt Della had purchased for her, the one most becoming to Hadley, and the only one she'd not yet worn: a gorgeous green wool. The weather certainly justified the heavy fabric, and she remembered then how Ari always loved her in this color. She plucked from her drawer her nicest brassiere, matching slip and the single pair of genuine silk stockings she owned and had for some reason been saving -- not even her wedding day deemed special enough to unwrap them for. Yet she got them out now and very carefully rolled them up her long legs.

Alright, what about the pearls? She decided in the end to wear them, (they certainly completed her stylish look), but what a slap in the face to Perry! Of course she wore her wedding band - she could not risk the appearance of going off without it - and Hadley reasoned to herself the jewelry demonstrated to Ari she was indeed valued, lest things somehow go awry again for the two of them and they instilled her with a sense of confidence she felt lacking throughout the harsh day. Outwardly she looked thoroughly captivating, while inside of Hadley raged a fury, her stomach maintaining the sensation of being on a terrifying carnival ride that wouldn't stop.

Would it EVER be six o'clock?

Chapter Seventeen

She closed the door to the house on Bagby, went down its front steps and thus began for Hadley an irreversible walk away from her childhood, from everything she had ever been taught about the difference between right and wrong. Remarkably, she did not encounter a single soul on her way to Hough Ranch and the evening, already haunting in its blackness - the frigid temperature causing her breath to look like vapors - felt like Halloween. It was so eerily quiet that with each footstep she could hear the crunch of gravel under her shoes and liked this sound, felt calmed by it and became less nervous, the emotion replaced now by excitement. She was getting closer.

Well, there Ari was in front of the iron gates of Hough, just as he had promised, the glow of his cigarette lighting the remainder of the way for her. Hadley gasped. He was really, truly there for her and she was really, truly doing this. He dropped the cigarette, crushing its butt with his heel and ran toward her, scooping her up in his arms like a bride being carried over the threshold.

"HADLEY!" he cried. "Beautiful, Perfect, Exquisite Hadley, you are here - at last!" he spun her around and around before he eventually set her down, crushing her into his arms in an enormous bear hug. "Oh my God, you smell SO GOOD!" He exclaimed into the back of her neck and she felt it then: a wetness trailing from the top of her spine, and it might have given her a chill, except it demonstrated Ari had been crying. He must want her as much as she wanted him and his tears were all the reassurance she needed. She would no longer be afraid of this spooky night, or their actions, or the liability. She was finally coming home and it was the single best moment of her life. The past few days had dragged on like molasses -- well, as far as Hadley was concerned, from this point forward the evening could not go slowly enough for the two of them.

He took her hand, that knuckle-to-knuckle basket grip she loved so much, and led her by the stone walls with iron plates that were now inscribed with 'HOUGH' and 'RANCH', and through the massive gates; she liked the creaking sound they made as he parted them, then in the direction of the big red barn - *of course*. She noticed as they got closer it had a large white star painted on it, front and center. Ari trailed Hadley's gaze to see what was beguiling her, brought his head close to her ear and explained,

"For Father. Earl and the fellows painted it... they wanted to honor his memory".

"An homage". Hadley declared in a quiet voice. "How lovely".

"Are you hungry, Hadley?"

Actually, she was starving! Inside the barn, she observed straight away that her man had been very thoughtful in planning their evening together: there was a lavish picnic dinner set up with a checkered blanket beneath it over a bale of hay for a makeshift table, and two more on either end for stools. Several small lambent lanterns were arranged in a circle around their festivities. Besides these provisions were a stack of blankets, his cello and, to Haley's delight, a collection of funny papers. (One of the best things Ari used to do was sit with Hadley's head in his lap and read her the funnies as he made up the cleverest voices, perfectly befitting each character). Oh, how she'd missed this simple, treasured pastime.

And there were violets.

Ari tried to pull out her 'chair' for her and wrapped a pink mohair blanket about her shoulders before he settled himself on the bale across from Hadley. He had wine for the two of them already poured and lifted his goblet:

"To Hadley, my future wife and partner in crime... and to the glorious life we will make together". They clinked glasses.

"To My Harry. And to Us. May we never, ever, be separated again and may we forevermore be happy and in love with each other. Eternally".

Ari beamed at her. He set down his wine and reached across the 'table' for her face, taking it in his hands so very tenderly. Reverently. He kissed her then... slowly, warmly. Finally! It felt to Hadley that she had had to live a lifetime since their last kiss -- and yet in equal measure, it felt like they had never been apart.

"You are the most remarkable creature I have ever laid my eyes upon. I want to ravage you!" His eyes blazed.

"Then you shall have to ravage me", she replied seductively, raising her arms in the air, "I am yours to do with what you want".

"I want... everything!"

Chapter Eighteen

"...But first, I am going to play my cello for you -- just as I promised the last time I escorted you home." Ari got up and reached for the massive wooden instrument which, despite its size and weight, was a true extension of himself. He played quietly... splendidly... exquisitely, for his audience of one. In spite of the chill Hadley melted. She rose from her bale stool, slipped the soft blanket from her shoulders and began to dance for him, slowly at first, for this musician before her who was the only man she had ever wanted to love her. Ari was absolutely perfect: mysterious, yet familiar. Romantic, yet goofy. Challenging, yet accepting. Soulful, yet light-hearted. She loved every single thing about her 'Harry', (including his last name, which sounded so lovely after her first: Hadley Hough), and felt a fullness in her heart that made it ache, but in a good way. She closed her eyes and swayed to the rhythm of his song, becoming lost in its melody.

At some point Ari stopped playing and stood to dance with his beauty. The pair had never before danced together, (though Hadley on her own was known for a fierce, prize-winning Charleston), and naturally they made such a graceful, fetching couple; all the music they had ever needed was between themselves. They were kissing now... deeply... hungrily, and with a passion they no longer felt compelled to repress. Ari's kisses went from her mouth to her neck and down to her breasts as he struggled to unbutton her blouse, while she was trying to undress him as well. Clumsy were the efforts of them both, but at last she was out of her brassiere and Ari fairly gasped when he saw her nakedness for the first time. She was breathtaking. Incandescent.

"You are the most beautiful woman I have ever seen, and I am done for!" he exclaimed.

And you are even more seductive and alluring then I ever imagined you could be.

Make love to me, Hadley!"

"I shall", she whispered.

Hadley had an innate sensuality about her -- she was aware of this, and she knew she had the goods to back it up. She sort of teased him then, playfully undressing the rest of the way. She wanted him to see she was capable of putting on a good show; she wanted him to remember this moment for the rest of their lives. He unbuckled his trousers and they came together, their coupling a sensation of smooth, skin to skin contact - finally - for the two of them. Still, they took their time, despite their carnal urges, and explored each other with their mouths... their tongues... their fingers... and they were creative, trying things that felt natural and titillating to them both, but erotic acts Hadley had never, ever heard about and things she wouldn't dare discuss with her friends -- and certainly never, ever with Lucille!

She would become his favorite instrument: her musician played Hadley expertly, to the point where she was humming, then singing, from the inside out. The ecstasy Ari brought to her made Hadley's entire body flush with warmth and quiver with pleasure; so THIS was what all the fuss was about. And he was tireless! The sensations he aroused in her were so overwhelming to Hadley, she had the evanescent thought they might be being watched -- but in the throes of her rapture, she couldn't have cared less. 'Let them watch me!' she dared. 'Who cares?' Certainly not these two lovers! They were in perfect harmony, theirs a concert which was a virtual explosion of gratification. Of bliss. They created their own universe there in the barn that bitter night and they did not want for anything but one another.

Afterward, Ari held his lady and showered her with kisses, covering every inch of Hadley's body with his appreciation. He declared his love for her over and over, and over again, belatedly remembering the two hot water bottles he'd brought to stave off the brisk temperature, and as he pulled them out something about this made him laugh - made them both laugh - and they laughed together until it hurt their bellies, yet it felt so satisfying. What a relief it was to release all this harnessed passion, the emotion and sheer joy of finally being together - and so totally.

"My Love, you must be starved by now!" Ari exclaimed.

Still overcome by their mirth, Hadley merely nodded.

He gathered a blanket around himself and got up to arrange a heaping plate of food: there was cheese and a thick slab of ham, (cold now, of course), soft bread and rhubarb pie for dessert, her favorite. Ari fed Hadley, kissed her on her mouth between spoonfuls, and fed her some more.

"I need to fortify you before Round Two!" he declared.

She giggled her approval. They just could not get enough of each other. And so it went, and on and on.

Eventually Ari lit a cigarette for them to share, they got out the rest of the blankets and made a provisional, yet snug bed. It was such a frigid night - but not for this couple. Ari nestled Hadley into his shoulder and massaged her head and neck until she was drowsy. Her eyes fluttered, she caught sight of the flickering lanterns and had a fleeting concern for their safety; she had occasionally had a bit of a premonition about being burned in a fire. But if they perished tonight, Hadley thought to herself, then she would die a completely happy, beloved woman and that was more than enough, at last, to lull her to sleep.

She awakened once sometime in the middle of the night and Ari sensed her arousal. He reached for his beauty, surprised she felt cold - while he was yet hot - and so he snuggled up behind her, encasing her form within his own and literally transferring his warmth to her body. He could feel himself cooling, as he could feel Hadley becoming warmer, and they fell back asleep this way - a consummate fit - his yin to her yang.

Chapter Nineteen

The Hough roosters crowed before dawn the following morning, their noises a harsh and menacing chorus. Reality announced itself with their discordant sounds and the lovers awoke in a panic. Whereas the previous evening they were all boldness and bravado, the prospect of now being discovered in their nakedness and invoking a scandal sobered the pair up in a hurry. Hadley dressed in haste, feeling a tension that made her anxious and verging on irritable. A quarrel threatened. Ari raked his long hair with his fingers as he rose from their cushy shelter. Could it be possible he was even MORE devastatingly handsome now that he'd taken her?

"What now, Ari?" Hadley asked, alarm in her voice. "What will be our next step?" She wanted answers. When he didn't reply, she became more agitated.

"Say something, Ari, or I am giving up on you!" she cried.

...And talk alone is not enough! Certainly we both know by now that words without actions are nothing more than empty air".

Ari buttoned his shirt as he thought for a moment, then decided:

"We will go to Perry first. And I will tell him you are leaving him for me, your true life mate, that we are restoring things back to their proper order. You and I were made for each other -- as any one of these townspeople can plainly see, including and especially Perry Wallace!"

"No!" Hadley fairly shouted, not appreciating how he'd brought Perry into it. "I will not agree to that! Perry has been nothing but a perfect gentleman and true friend to me, and the least I can do is to tell him myself... He deserves as much".

Ari became annoyed now as well. It seemed like they were both spoiling for a fight, the not-so-pretty aftermath of their duplicity.

"I do not want you with him, Hadley! I do not want to give him the chance to sway you!" His temper was rising.

"...Well, you have someone to speak to yourself. So while I am packing up my things at Bagby, you must tell your mother you and I are going to be together after all -- that wild horses couldn't keep you away from me!" she demanded. She was emphatic on this one point and would return to Perry otherwise.

"Of course I will say that to her, and a lot more. I told you by the bandstand: I will fight for you, Hadley! And if Mother does not give her approval to our union then we will leave Liberty at once... Maybe we should leave regardless.

We could go to New York, or even back to Chicago, so you can resume your studies at Northwestern. I am devoted to you Hadley -- and fully invested in making all your dreams come true".

She could see he meant every word of this and softened. He was right: they probably should leave Liberty and create a new life together somewhere else. Hadley didn't want their love for each other to always be tainted by scandal, when to her it felt so pure and natural.

But then she thought she heard voices, perhaps Earl and his farmhands so, quickly, she buttoned her coat and hastily wrapped her scarf about her neck. She had to get out of there now or engender certain discovery.

"I will drive you back to Bagby" Ari insisted, dropping the cigarette he'd just begun lighting.

"I don't know: do you think we can get to your roadster undetected?" his lover fretted. It would not do for anyone to find out about their affair before they had a chance to speak to the offended principle players themselves.

Without saying more, Ari grabbed her by the hand, then ducked out of the barn and down to where his automobile was parked. Still the attentive companion, he took time to hold open her door for Hadley and once they were settled inside his orange car, Ari adjusted her scarf, tenderly tucking it into her collar, and cupped her face with his hands. He locked eyes with his lady and stated,

"We can DO this, Hadley! I will let you off out of view of your neighbors, come back to Hough and await Mother's return from Wymore. After I have spoken with her I will come to collect you. Surely this will give you enough time to gather your things and make your peace with Perry.

I adore you, my soon-to-be-Mrs. Arlington Hough. Do you know how much? More than any man has ever loved a woman - of this you can be sure". *The last thing he did was to kiss my grandmother on the lips - firmly, fully - and she could feel his reassurance and passion for her. Something to hold onto...*

They arrived at Bagby Lane. Hadley closed the door to his Model-A as noiselessly as she could, cast a fugitive glance about the little neighborhood but did not dare look back at her lover, for fear of caving in from dread and the unpleasantness that undoubtedly awaited -- until she heard how his automobile had turned the corner. She looked over her shoulder and could see curls of exhaust dissipate and - poof! - Ari and his burnt orange roadster, not to mention its toffee-colored rumble seat, had vanished without a trace, much like a vivid dream where one awakens, cognizant they've been dreaming -- but strangely, almost instantly has no recollection of its substance whatsoever.

Still, she did have a dilatory realization that they hadn't thought to clean up their camp, the evidence of which would be in plain view for Earl and his boys. Too late now, however: it was time to face the music.

Chapter Twenty

Hadley had barely gotten through the door to Perry's home when she heard the dissonant sounds of the telephone. Was it her imagination, or were they announcing some sort of alarm bell for her? Her head throbbed, her ears buzzed, and she was tempted to ignore their penetrations. But no such luck for Hadley: Central was persistent.

"Hello, Central. Whoever could it be who wants to interrupt me so early on a Saturday morning?" Hadley inquired as she wrestled with her overcoat in an effort to free herself from the garment, but with one hand holding the receiver while trying to disrobe herself with the other, she struggled with the sleeves and barely masked the irritation and fatigue she felt in her voice, as well as in her body. There. She was out of it.

"Hadley! Central here". (As if she didn't know that). "You must get over to Fishback at once! I hate to have to tell you this, but there was a terrible accident at the farmhouse very early there this morning. Central was crying now.

"Your mama suffered some pretty bad burns to her arms and hands. But Hadley? Are you there, Hadley? I'm afraid to have to be the one to tell you... ... I am so terribly sorry, Hadley, but... Buddy didn't make it".

Hadley dropped the receiver, effectuating it to swing ominously back and forth, and ran out the front door without stopping to close it behind her. Central MUST be mistaken, grievously, HIDEOUSLY mistaken! How on EARTH could her darling girl, who for each one of her thirteen years had represented everything in life that was unadulterated, authentic and ethereal, possibly be gone without her sensing it? Surely if something had happened to Buddy, Hadley would have FELT it!

Too stunned or frightened to cry, (crying meant it was truly happening, and it could not TRULY be happening), she ran down Bagby Lane and toward the rural route as quickly as her legs could carry her - she HAD to get to her baby - but her stride was restricted by the slim cut of her skirt. She turned the corner to the highway, ears burning and heart pounding, as the phrase from Central replayed itself over and over again in her head. Hadley ran along this way for quite a spell, long enough for her shoes to fill with gravel and her feet to form the beginnings of painful, bloody blisters. Despite the chilly temperature and lack of her overcoat, she was perspiring heavily by the time Clyde Rayfield, Papa's closest friend and the man who did the milking and had been filling in for her at the dairy, pulled up abruptly beside her in the Model-T.

"Honey! Get in!" he shouted. "I've come to take you to Fishback".

"Clyde!" She prevailed upon him. "Please tell me Buddy is alright!" This HAD to be a very bad dream.

Hadley struggled trying to climb into the old truck in her narrow skirt. Clyde assisted her and gave her hand a firm squeeze.

"I'm so sorry, Hon-" he attempted, but then his voice broke.

There was far too much pressure in her head and chest, yet - somehow - she managed to ask him what had happened.

"Buddy was sent to that new store just past daybreak to get a pint of kerosene for the kitchen stove, only they must have sold her gasoline instead. When she tried to light it, the gasoline was too volatile, vapor ignited and it caused a terrible explosion. She was killed instantly". He was crying openly now, wiping his nose with his kerchief unselfconsciously and heaving deep, anguished sobs. "I just pray she didn't suffer. I can't stand to think of it... she was the sweetest, cheeriest, most wonderful girl".

Hadley couldn't stand it either! This could not actually be happening; she must be trapped in a horrific nightmare! She could not - WOULD NOT - go on without the light of her life and felt her conscience crowding her, encroaching upon her thoughts -- and combating her with the brutal truth that had she not been so selfish and so immoral, her cherished Buddy would be here at this very moment, alive and unscathed. Oh, she was the most sinister of all the world's traitors! How would she ever endure these glaring realities, about her sister's tragic death and her undeniable culpability?

Clyde squealed into Fishback and Hadley could see plumes of charcoal smoke emanating from the farmhouse as well as the undertaker's portentous black wagon. She wrestled with the door of the truck, breaking free as quickly as she could and running at a sprint to get inside and to her precious girl. Neighbors were on the premises, throwing buckets of water at the side of the house, embers continuing to burn. There was shouting and commotion; morbid pandemonium.

Inside their home she saw that the parlor doors were open - normally this part of the house would be closed off until next springtime - and their town physician, Doc Bachle, between the piano and library table built by her papa, kneeling next to the davenport attending Hadley's mama, who was seated there, bandaging her arms and hands and speaking to her very softly. The atmosphere was hazy and foul-smelling and she was assaulted by its rancid stench; a combination of smoke, water and caustic ash. The environment was alternately jarringly chaotic then freakishly quiet. Hadley rushed from one downstairs room to another in search of Buddy - no amount of smoke or noxious odor, or trepidation of what her sister's condition might appear as, would keep her from her angel - yet couldn't find her.

"WHERE IS BUDDY?" She demanded. "I WANT MY SISTER! I NEED TO SEE HER!" She gave into hysteria then, but her tirade was interrupted by the mournful wails of her papa, whom in her entire life had never shed a single tear that she was aware of, and the plaintive cries coming from this man were the most pitiful noises she had ever heard, excruciating to her ears, which seemed to still be filled with blood and heat and pressure. Then Perry arrived in his Chevrolet, screeching to an abrupt stop just before the front porch, his driving too swift and haphazard. He slammed the car door and began shouting her name from outside of the house.

Before she knew it he had rushed to her side, overwhelming Hadley with his presence. Dear God! Another layer of dread for her -- and another confrontation to her conscience.

"Hadley! Are you alright? I was so worried about you!" he exclaimed, reaching for his bride.

"Perry!" She cried as she searched his eyes. "Don't you know? It is Buddy! They say she is *dead*!"

Perry looked at her as though he did not understand what she was telling him. It felt like everything was in S - L - O – W motion and for one long, agonizing moment he did not comprehend the English language.

"But how could this have happened? Weren't you with her, Hadley? I thought you spent the night at Fishback to keep Buddy company". He was so confused. Guileless.

Mama glanced up from Doc Bachle's ministrations. In spite of her compromised hearing, she had somehow interpreted their conversation. She studied her daughter, prolongedly, defiantly... accusingly. Then she spoke for the first time in over a year.

"*Florence*!"

Just one word. But to Hadley it told volumes of her knowledge about her middle daughter's treachery. It was her way of telling Hadley that Buddy was hers, had always belonged to her, and never to Hadley. This single name scraped at Hadley's very soul as only her mother, of all people, could penetrate, (*our parents seem to reach the deepest part of us, do they not?),* and tore her conscience wide open. She started to scream - or was it Hadley who screamed - and did not stop, the gut-wrenching lamentations drowning out everything else. Perry, and perhaps Papa, tried to comfort her then, but it was all too much for Hadley. The room began to spin and then

everything went dark.

PART TWO

"What happens in Nebraska, stays in Nebraska... too bad nothing ever happens in Nebraska" ~ my mother's favorite coffee mug

Chapter Twenty-One

Hadley woke up back in her marriage bed and when she opened her eyes there was Doc Bachle, Perry, Papa - even Aunt Della - all surrounding their girl. Doc spoke to her first.

"Hadley, can you hear me? It's Doc Bachle, Hadley, and I gave you a sedative to help you sleep. You've suffered an unimaginable loss, but you are going to be alright. Can you say something, Hadley?"

Nothing.

"Hadley! Can you see who's here with me? Can you tell me who you know?"

When Hadley didn't answer, Perry piped up.

"Hadley, it's me, Perry. Your husband! You are in our bedroom, at our home on Bagby Lane."

Hadley looked from one person to the next, searching their faces, but did not register recognition of any of them - not even her papa. She seemed disoriented, and very far away. Perry wondered aloud what was wrong with his new wife. Doc Bachle opened his black leather medical bag and proceeded to examine his as-yet-unresponsive patient.

"Hadley is evidently in shock", Doc pronounced after shining a light in both of her eyes, "and she is going to need far more care than I can provide for her here. I strongly urge you to consider a psychiatric hospital or a sanitarium".

"You don't think she is just terribly sad, distraught over..." this from Papa, who could not bear to lose another daughter.

"I think she needs good, comprehensive psychiatric care," Doc interrupted, "And I am not equipped or qualified to administer it to her. I know you do not want to lose another daughter, Ismay". Doc seemed to have read the poor man's mind. "I also realize we are in the midst of a Depression, and this kind of hospitalization does not come cheap".

Aunt Della now:

"I will pay for whatever my niece requires... it is the least I can do", she declared. Always dainty and pretty, the lady appeared doleful, to have suddenly aged ten years.

"That is very good of you, Della, but Hadley is my wife and I will take responsibility for her treatment, Thank-you all the same" stated Perry. He turned to the doctor. "Doc, do you think you can make the necessary arrangements?"

Doc studied the bespectacled husband.

"I do, Perry. You are a good man, a brave one. I know a similarly honest, trustworthy fellow, a Doctor Paul Prentiss of Wichita Kansas. I'd like to send Hadley to him. He and his father have a sanitarium there, and Paul specializes in psychoanalysis. I trust him and believe he can supervise her recovery". Doc looked at them each, these aggrieved and unfortunate family members.

"You have, all of you, endured the worst kind of tragedy possible, and I want to stop the bleeding, so-to-speak; I want this young woman restored to you, and your family healed. Please excuse me now, so I can finish my examination of Hadley in private, then I will wire Dr. Prentiss".

The three complied with Doc's wishes, promptly stepping out of the young couple's bedroom, and Perry went a step further - onto his front porch. This was an awful lot of reality for one twenty-eight-year-old newlywed man to take on and he needed a moment alone to gather his thoughts. Outside, however, he spotted Ari in the yard leaning against his flashy orange roadster, one foot resting on a running board, his arms folded in support, as a pillow, behind his head. When he saw Perry, he took it as an invitation to approach the house and hurried up their short walkway.

Perry confronted him from the top of his steps:

"What do you want here, Hough? What are you doing on my property?" For the first time since he'd lived in the little bungalow, Perry acted territorial.

"I have been waiting for over three days to see Hadley - I heard the sorrowful news about Buddy - and I have come to check on her and pay my respects".

Perry started toward him.

"Then go out to Fishback and offer your condolences. Bertha is at the farm, Lucille as well; maybe even Herbert has arrived by now. The wake is morning after tomorrow", he said, his voice rising.

"I will go over to Fishback, but I'd like to visit Hadley first - "

"Why?" Perry challenged him, putting hands on his hips as he sized up his potential rival. He had always been good with numbers and the last time he'd checked, one plus one still equaled two. Now he was starting to put two and two together -- and the sum total he arrived at infuriated Perry. He had the sudden urge to pummel Ari, right there in front of his house!

"Because I care about her!" Ari shouted. "Very much. Hadley and I have been... friends, since we were youngsters."

"She won't know who you are", Perry retorted. "She doesn't even recognize her own father! She's in pretty rough shape, actually". Hadley's new husband suddenly looked deflated.

Ari tried to brush past him, but either Doc Bachle had heard the shouting and commotion or had finished his examination; one way or another he was on the porch now as well intercepting the hotheaded fellow and reiterating everything Perry had just said -- effectively putting another wall between any dreams of a future for the star-crossed couple.

"Young Hough! I advise against your going inside. Hadley is in a precarious state, hanging in the balance if you must know. I've just given her another sedative and hopefully by the time she wakes up she will be in the Prentiss Sanitarium in Wichita, Kansas.

If you truly care about her then stay out of the way and let the experts do their job".

Ari's every instinct told him to remain - that the love of his life would indeed be revived by him - yet adrenaline from a potential fight with Perry was coursing through his veins and his body felt less certain. He was a little shaky from nerves and lack of sleep, so Hadley's lover vacillated.

After a few awkward moments he finally asked the doctor,

"Is she going to be alright?"

"That remains to be seen. I pray so.

If you care for Hadley and her well-being then pray for her, Ari, and pray for the Palmer family. Pray for them all... and please just leave them be".

Chapter Twenty-Two

December 28th, 1931: Prentiss Sanitarium, Wichita, Kansas. Hadley Palmer Wallace had been a patient there for over two months now... and she wasn't getting any better. She had missed Buddy's funeral, the Halloween and Thanksgiving holidays, as well as Christmastime -- not to mention Ari's business school graduation from Doane. During the daytime she stayed in a fetal position or when prone, rocked herself back and forth. At night she slept fitfully, if at all. She barely ate and spoke even less. She'd become alarmingly gaunt and developed dark circles under her eyes. Her hair was wild. Hadley suffered a broken heart the day her younger sister died -- somehow and nonetheless, her heart continued on beating.

Dr. Prentiss was at a loss as to how to proceed with his very sad and oddly guilt-ridden patient. Her care was too costly for Perry and his mother; they were running out of money. Marguerite Wallace had been forced to sell her home in Beatrice and was planning to move west to California and live with Perry's older brother Albertus and his little family.

During their sessions Dr. Prentiss tried to delve into Hadley's family history and relationship patterns, but the most she was able to confide to him was, “Love hurts”. Or, “It hurts too much to love”. Having no knowledge of Ari - and Hadley’s mortal shame over her affair with him - the psychiatrist naturally assumed she meant it hurt too much to love, then lose, her baby sister. He did not think she suffered from unrest of the spirit as much she suffered from genuine heartbreak -- and unfortunately he did not have a panacea for that.

He liked the Wallaces, particularly Perry, and did not want to waste their time and resources such as they were. Perry and Marguerite were in his office now and it was time for a frank discussion:

“Good Afternoon, Mr. and Mrs. Wallace”, he began. “Please sit down. Mildred is getting tea for you both. And when she returns, I fear I must give you the unvarnished truth in regards to Hadley and her progress here at Prentiss Sanitarium”.

The two looked at the good doctor solemnly, then at one another. Obediently they awaited his report. Mildred came in with a tray of tea and some ginger cookies. A warm fire snapped and burned in a cozy corner fireplace. The surroundings were pleasant, homey even; the words coming from the psychiatrist however, were not.

“I submit to you both, regrettably so, that I am making very little progress with the younger Mrs. Wallace. She is not subject to fits of temper

- certainly has never been violent - and her unrest of spirit is entirely understandable given the traumatic event she endured. Yet she has not really opened up to me -- and while it is no crime against her sanity not to want to talk about something too painful, if I cannot get her to confide in me, I really cannot help her any further.

... I wish I had the capability of destroying this past unfavorable memory which seems to have seized your young wife, but that is not feasible - not in this country, anyway. Other than managing her bereavement, I do not know what else we have to offer her here.

And I wonder if it wouldn't be better for her to be back in her familiar surroundings now with the people who know and care about her most. She will likely remain sad for a while and much quieter than you are accustomed to, but I do not believe she is a mortal danger to herself."

Perry and his mother exchanged a long look as they considered the doctor's words. While anxious to be relieved of the tremendous financial strain containing Hadley was costing them, they were likewise nervous about assuming full responsibility for her. When it came right down to it Perry had to admit that he didn't know his new wife very well -- and certainly not the grievously lonesome young woman Dr. Prentiss just described. Marguerite had never actually met her. Happy New Year.

Chapter Twenty-Three

And so in early 1932 Perry escorted his dour bride back to Liberty, Nebraska and back to their little house on Bagby Lane. During the long drive he tried to make small talk - about Marguerite's impending move west to California, Albertus' two young boys and some of their more amusing shenanigans, the bleak January weather - all to no avail. Hadley sat in his Chevrolet in stony silence and stared straight ahead, her only concession accepting the occasional Lucky Strike cigarette he offered her. She had deep circles under her eyes and looked as though she hadn't taken a comb to her hair since she'd been sent to Prentiss. Unkempt. That was the word that came to mind for Perry when he collected her. Oh, how he missed his spirited wife! The dismal weather seemed to match his outlook and Perry wondered, more than once, if he would see the vibrant female he had been so taken with ever again.

When they got to the little bungalow she could tell there had been some changes to the place and Perry ascertained as much, explaining that Bertha and Ismay had been living with him while the damaged farmhouse underwent its reparations. Maybe it was a recollection of the side of her childhood home up in ghastly flames or perhaps hearing her mother's first name spoken aloud, whatever the case, Hadley sort of snapped out of her funk then and began to respond to him. She did have a conscience after all, as well as a raw sense of self-preservation. She knew how fortunate she was to have Perry and the umbrella of protection he offered her; she also knew how close she came to losing him, via her mother's confession. She was going to have to be very, very careful and very, very grateful. He couldn't touch her heart - she didn't think she had one anymore - but he could be allowed to touch her body. It was early in a long mid-western wintertime, it was the midst of the Great Depression, and a man such as Perry had few creature comforts in his life. She HAD to become - and remain - one of them.

"Hadley Dear, are you hungry for some supper?" Perry wondered, as he peered into the ice box. Bertha had been thoughtful to leave some provisions for the couple's homecoming and Perry began to move about the kitchen and make a simple meal.

"...Actually, Perry, I'm more thirsty than hungry; what say we go to Lou Lu's for a drink or two?"

He was taken by surprise at her request, and it stopped him in his tracks: It felt unseemly to Perry that they should be out drinking and carousing so soon after her arrival home from the sanitarium, (not to mention the morbid event that triggered her stay there), and he tried to dissuade his confounding wife.

"A drive then?" She suggested.

Unbelievable. (How come every word he now associated with Hadley began with 'un'?) He thought she must be kidding: they had only just come in from a tedious and somber - at least for him - drive from Wichita.

"Let's have some Dinner and maybe listen to a radio show instead; I believe "Amos 'n' Andy" is on this evening. And I know your pals Thelma and Bess are itching to stop by and pay you a visit. How does that sound?"

'Dull as dishwater', Hadley mumbled under her breath.

Chapter Twenty-Four

Normalcy. It was what Perry wanted more than anything and the one thing that eluded him. He tried to be as helpful as he could to Hadley, making up their bed before he left for work each day - if she was actually out of bed - and fixing coffee for the two of them. He was tidy and considerate and took care of his own things. He offered to drive her out to Fishback to see Missy and her folks; he suggested she go to Donna Dee's for a new hair-do; he arranged a game of bridge with some of her old friends. He brought books from the local library and did their grocery shopping after his Saturday morning pay. Money was tight, to be sure - as small a thing as a tomato they'd have to wait to buy until he'd been paid - but Perry kept his worries about their finances to himself. And he never, ever, brought up the subject of Buddy or what had happened at the farm that funereal day back in October... and Hadley didn't either.

She was still eager to go out in the evenings, especially to Lou Lu's. Perry dodged her overtures as well as he could - it seemed indecent to him, unwholesome, actually -- (un, un, un, un, UN!) - so finally one Saturday Hadley got a notion in her head that they should drive to Beatrice instead and have a drink and a smoke at the Green Lantern Inn. When Perry would not oblige her request she began to pout, eventually going out to the Chevrolet and sitting inside the passenger seat of the car. She sat there very still and remained that way for several hours. *And it became a pattern for my Grandma. I remember her doing this several times when we were on vacation at our family's lake home and my dad had offended her.*

Perry honestly did not know how to please his shadowy bride... except in the bedroom of all places. There she was strangely responsive - aggressive even. Truth be told, her appetite for this particular marital activity bordered on the voracious. One evening when Perry came in after an unusually long day on the job Hadley was already in their room, suggestively sprawled out on the bed. As soon as he entered she asked,

"Hey Mister, how 'bout a roll in the hay?"

He was aroused by her - of course - but also a little spooked: he'd never known a nice girl to be the seductress, and certainly not his wife! Naturally their frequent couplings, many times without the use of a sheath, resulted in a pregnancy fairly quickly.

Right around Valentine's Day Hadley learned from Doc Bachle she was with child. Doc was more than a little concerned by this development, Perry wasn't sure how they would manage, and her girlfriends questioned Hadley's stability. But she surprised them all - even Papa and Aunt Della - and took to the news and subsequent changes in her body quite naturally. She consulted Doc Bachle on any number of questions and concerns and treated his wisdom as gospel. She was going to be a mother now; Hadley had a new purpose.

Chapter Twenty-Five

For the next few months it seemed to her family and friends that they'd gotten their old Hadley back, and then some. She ate well, napped or took walks in the afternoons with her friends, and started to set up a little nursery. The extra weight and rest became her; Hadley was thriving. The Palmers were buoyed by the news their middle daughter was expecting and Bertha, whose hands and arms had finally healed, made tiny baby clothes. Plus, it was springtime.

One splendid day in June when she was about five months along, Hadley's childhood friends, Thelma and Bess, treated her to a small shopping spree in Beatrice. The trio was lively and chatty and had the nicest time choosing some sweet but inexpensive items, taking Hadley to high tea at the Paddock Hotel and linking arms, three in a row, as they window shopped. It was the best she had felt in a very long time. Back in Liberty by early evening, Hadley wanted to continue their celebration.

Perry was up in Omaha on business, her girlfriends had long gone home, but still she was restless. Hadley surveyed herself in their bedroom's full-length mirror and decided she didn't look too plump yet to go out on the town;

she was craving a little action. So she changed into a light blue print and finger-curled her hair, adding lipstick and a bit of rouge, and as a final touch, fastened the pearls about her neck. She had so much energy lately, she could have walked to Lou Lu's - the weather was certainly cooperative - but Papa had recently loaned her the Model-T, aware that Perry was sometimes away and an expectant mother might have an unexpected need of transportation.

She started up the old truck and headed toward the familiar speakeasy, feeling optimistic. It was filled with patrons and gaiety and Hadley was glad for it, thought she might blend into the crowd and people-watch for a while. She scooted up on a bar stool a bit awkwardly and ordered her favorite bootleg beer. She told Lou to put it on Perry's tab. He lit a cigarette for her as he proffered her a smile and some peanuts, the shells of which - along with a layer of sawdust - were scattered on the tavern floor, and encouraged Hadley to stay for the live music. She looked around to see who else was there. As she was licking the last of the foam from the top of her drink, Hadley thought she overheard Vernon Bowhay boasting about his new steer. Typical male, status-oriented conversation, she said to herself. Boring. She was on the verge of tuning him out when she caught the phrase,

"...Can you beat it? Ari Hough and Priscilla Barneston! Talk about a merger; Widow Hough must be rubbing her hands together at the thought of all that money!"

Hadley felt suddenly, overwhelmingly, sick-to-her-stomach -- and not from the baby inside her womb. Apparently there was something left of her battered heart because the pain emanating from her chest had become so excruciating, she was desperate to get out of the now-hostile-seeming speakeasy before she truly embarrassed herself. Lou asked after her as she abruptly got up from her stool, practically knocking it over, but she ignored the bartender and bolted from the tavern before he could check on her any further. She brushed past a couple on their way in; the woman had both of her arms locked possessively, like a chain link, around her escort's elbow, the man appeared quite handsome and sure of himself. She had the desultory impulse to scream at the two of them,

"*Don't be fooled by love*! *Run while you can*!"

By the time she'd made it to the Model-T, Hadley was in tears, her entire body shaking. All these months she had pushed Ari from her thoughts as far as she could, yet hearing about him now - and in such a cavalier way - felt nothing short of cruel. It wasn't as if she entertained romantic fantasies -- any fanciful thinking or dreaming on her part had perished in that gruesome fire along with Buddy. But to know he was doing his own thing and doing so well for himself - engaged to a wealthy socialite -

was just too much for this eighteen-year-old woman to bear. She had been sent to the brink by Buddy's death and could ill-afford another setback.

The temperature was warm and inviting, the sky was alive with stars that evening -- and still it was the darkest, most palpably lonely night of Hadley's life. She ACHED from missing her darling sister - as though Buddy were somehow up there along with the stars and the moon, yet utterly out of reach - just like any future between her and Ari. They were phantoms, she realized, the both of them: her pet sister, whose love for her had been the deepest, least complicated emotion Hadley had ever known, and her 'Harry', (what good was it, she wondered, to experience a passion so fierce and all-encompassing, only to have to learn to live without it -- when it was the single time in her life she had understood what it meant to feel truly alive?)

Carousers and revelers came and went, oblivious to the disconsolate young woman, and she to them, as Hadley sat inside that truck with her head against the steering wheel and her shoulders heaving - heart searing - and cried as she had never cried before from some primal place within herself. She cried for Buddy and her lost future, begging with God to please, let her come back! She wailed for Ari and the loss of their sweet and initially uncorrupted love, wishing fervently she could turn back the hands of time to when he belonged to her and she was whole and happy.

Hadley cried so hard she couldn't catch her breath and felt more alone than she ever had, despite the tiny baby growing inside her. She was inconsolable, even to herself. It is hard to say how long she remained like this, but by the time she finally started up the engine, she was virtually blinded by her own tears. She somehow put the truck into gear and began to head away from the parking lot of Lou Lu's, yet the tears would not stop flowing and this young mother-to-be couldn't see - most significantly the large oak tree just ahead of her, one of the only ones at Liberty's outskirts - and drove straight into it, full stop. The Model-T was spewing steam, its front end smashed into the shape of an accordion, engine ruined; her face slammed hard against the steering wheel. Hadley was bleeding and then unconscious.

...But Thank Goodness the fetus inside her womb was unharmed, because that delicate life was my father, and he would be coming to this world with a beautiful mind - a chemical genius.

After the car accident Grandma had a scar over her left eye for the rest of her life.

Chapter Twenty-Six

Back in the hospital. Only this time, not for psychiatric treatment. When Hadley demolished Papa's old Model-T she banged herself up pretty badly in the bargain: along with a deep gash to her forehead, she suffered a few broken ribs and a fairly serious concussion. Doc Bachle sewed up her forehead and gave morphine for the painful ribs, but he was worried about her concussion, particularly in light of Hadley's recent struggles. He advised a stay in the hospital up in Lincoln, 'at least for observation, if not peace of mind'. Naturally he was worried about her unborn child. It didn't take long for the news of Hadley's automobile accident to spread through Liberty, courtesy of Central. Perry was beginning to associate calls from the operator with bad news and started to dread answering the telephone -- all the more so if he was away from his wife. By the time he had been notified of Hadley's latest calamity Aunt Della had as well, and she brooked no argument in assuming financial responsibility for her mired niece. When she finally spoke to Perry by long-distance, she was adamant:

"This time there is another life involved - and future kin to me; I want reassurance Hadley's baby is going to be alright. Don't argue with me, Perry. It is impolite to argue with an old person!"

"You are hardly old, Della", Perry chuckled, "But thank-you very kindly just the same. Your help is most appreciated. Times sure are tough around here... I imagine you are sorely needing a vacation from the various hardships of your family".

At her offer, Aunt Dee could hear the relief in Perry's voice. "Will do, soon enough" she responded from her end of the receiver. "And actually I am thinking of moving to Colorado, to the Rocky Mountains and clean mountain air now that Lucille has finished school. But a new life will breathe joy into this entire family -- which may have to be holiday enough for me, at least for the time being".

Della told him then of her plans to come to Liberty for the months of July and August. She would be a calm, steadying presence for Hadley and the Palmers, and she was always good company. Perry brightened. Hadley mended and expanded. Between her protective husband and concerned family and friends, she was almost never left alone for the remainder of that summer. They did their best to boost her spirits and abide the relentless heat, (some days so hot you could honestly fry an egg right there on the sidewalk), and near-suffocating humidity.

And then the letters started coming.

Chapter Twenty-Seven

I know what you did in the barn. Does your husband know?

...Would you like him to??

Hadley looked at the note in her hands and started trembling, her fingers shaking. Was someone ACTUALLY trying to blackmail her? And for what purpose? She could not distinguish whether it was male or female handwriting - Miss Linley had excelled at instructing her students toward a perfect, uniform cursive - and the stationary it was written on was plain, white -- no letterhead or monogram by which to individuate its author. Hadley wracked her brain as she tried to think of who could be so vicious to want to put such fear in her, a now nineteen-year-old mother-to-be without any means to speak of, swollen with child and still emotionally vulnerable.

The letter did not ask for money, so what was its intent? She wondered. Obviously she could not show the contents to anyone, let alone reveal her affair with Ari to them. Upon further reflection, Hadley recalled that one time last April she had received a little note which simply stated '*Adultery is a Sin*'. She did not put much stock in it at the time; it wasn't addressed to her specifically and she'd chalked it up to some religious zealot who may have very well put such a phrase in everybody's mailbox, for all she knew. But clearly she'd been wrong! And make no mistake about it: this letter was meant for her, and her alone.

She paced the little house - waddled was more like it - as her fear burgeoned. She could not risk Perry finding out, especially now, in the final stage of her pregnancy... and after all she'd put him through. Were he to learn of this he would quickly deduce she wasn't worth all the trouble, and Hadley would be damaged goods -- no better than poor Betty Jo Svoboda and her little daughter Agnes. And what would become of their baby? He or she would not be a bastard - technically, no – but might Perry reject a child borne after an adulterous act even if that child were clearly his? How would Hadley manage then? She would not! Not without a job or a degree or any kind of savings. Not in this seemingly endless Depression...

If possible, she felt more isolated in their stuffy furnace box of a front room than she had that night in the Model-T outside of Lou Lu's, and determined then she must stick closer to home, at least for the rest of her confinement. She shuddered as she closed the curtains - something she had never before done during the daytime, no matter what the weather - and though the walls of the little bungalow now seemed to be closing in on her, Hadley felt a fear more keenly than her claustrophobia; she was suddenly afraid of everyone - including her own shadow. Her life was shrinking by the minute, even as her belly enlarged. Then the baby kicked and brought her back to reality.

Hadley studied the letter more carefully and noticed something she hadn't picked up on before: after the second question, the author of the note had placed two question marks in a row. Peculiar. That said something of his, (or her), character, didn't it? She had a funny feeling then, a sort of female intuition: could it be Ari's mother who was menacing her? Could it be Marion Hough??

Chapter Twenty-Eight

Three more hand written letters:

Fornicator!!!

Sinners burn in Hell!

You may be married to a saint, but you are as bad as the Devil Himself.

...Three more days where Hadley stayed indoors.

Chapter Twenty-Nine

By September Aunt Della had returned to Chicago, where she indeed began to prepare for a move to the rocky mountains of Colorado. Lucille might as well have played musical chairs with her aunt because no sooner did Della arrive back in the windy city than Hadley's older sister came to Liberty for a short stay.

It was during harvest time for the corn crop and while farmers were busy in their fields from dawn until dusk, the womenfolk took advantage of their men's absence to catch up on some quilting and gossiping. The Liberty Quilting Society held a few bees that month, the last and largest at the First Congregational Church. Bertha stayed on the fringes of any organized social activities and remained at home but with her oldest daughter visiting, sensitive to her mama's probable exclusion and definite isolation, Lucille declared that they should have a small get-together of their own out at Fishback, a knitting bee with Hadley as the guest of honor! So she invited Hadley's girlfriends Thelma and Bess, along with Betty Jo Svoboda and her mother Eunice, and made up some dainty refreshments and sweet iced tea.

The day of the gathering the seven ladies sat in a circle in the parlor room of the old farmhouse eating finger sandwiches and deviled eggs, drinking sweet tea and making quiet conversation as they pieced together a baby blanket for Hadley's unborn son. It was a pleasant enough, if somewhat sluggish afternoon, but Hadley appreciated her sister's efforts -- and especially her it's-us-against-world mentality, which was something new for Lucille.

Actually, she had been very solicitous of Hadley since she'd arrived into town, much to her expectant sister's dismay and of course her great relief. (This was the first time the two had seen each other since the tragic accident and Lucille had been so kind and considerate toward Hadley, she seriously contemplated confiding in her all about the devastating affair with Ari and subsequent threatening letters, despite her sister's previous lack of sympathy -- and the fact that Lucille could never before keep a secret even if her life depended on it).

But she had always been fastidious and organized to the point of compulsion, so it came as no surprise that during her visit Lucille had undertaken the grim task of cleaning out Buddy's and Hadley's old bedroom. Just as the women were collecting purses and gloves and saying their 'good-byes', she brought out a little bundle of Buddy's prized artwork for them to admire. They set down their things so they might "ooh" and "aah" over her various sketches and drawings with charming little bubble captions, and agreed, albeit in hushed, somber tones that the youngster had possessed genuine talent.

A few of the pictures were of a man and woman enjoying a campfire, sitting in a small row boat and fishing on a lake. Lucille speculated, a bit too loudly, that these drawings were perhaps meant to be depictions of Hadley and Perry on their honeymoon trip to Burntside Lodge. At this query from her older sister - this vocal pronouncement - Hadley thought she might really and truly lose her mind, because, of course they were! And in that awful moment, Hadley believed, once again, that she could not trust Lucille whatsoever -- and wondered if the sole purpose of the party was to psychologically sabotage her. Lucille was obviously aware of these illustrations before the guests arrived, and she HAD to have known how unsettling this 'discovery' would be for her expectant sister.

Horror-struck, Hadley realized the pictures were drawn after her final conversation with Buddy, the one where she'd told her all about Lake Burntside and what sort of things she and Perry had done there for their amusement. Her beloved girl must have fashioned this magazine as a special handmade offering, expecting Hadley to come to Fishback that fateful evening and aware she was bringing Buddy a postcard and some moccasins, it would have been just like the thirteen-year-old to want to reciprocate with a gift of her own.

Consternation and a fresh tide of guilt coursed over Hadley's entire body until she was chilled to the very bone. It was as if a hand from the grave had risen up, pointing a macabre finger at her, (or was it in fact Lucille's finger?), and letting Hadley, as well as the other ladies - as her older sibling made very clear - know for certain she had betrayed the one who idolized her, depended on her and loved her unconditionally, all in the name of lust, and with the direst of consequences. The afternoon ruined, she lamely excused herself, made haste out of Fishback, drove home in the Chevy and got into bed... then remained there.

It is how Perry found his expectant wife and he was at a loss as to how to comfort her. So he climbed under the sheets along with Hadley - and held on for dear life.

Chapter Thirty

Somehow it was finally October 31st - Halloween - 1932: my father's birthday. Hadley and her husband welcomed their infant son into their little family and decided to name him Perry Junior, or 'PJ', as he came to be known. He easily favored the Wallace side of the family save for his coloring and almond-shaped eyes, which appeared to be lit from within just like his mother's: *the smiling eyes of my grandma.*

PJ was a relatively easy baby and Hadley doted on her first child. All the caring and protectiveness she had instinctively felt for her younger sister were transferred now to her little boy and he thrived in her care... some would even suggest that PJ was spoiled. (For a long time he slept in the same bedroom as his parents and when he woke up in the morning PJ, while still in his crib, liked to throw an empty bottle at his mother's head; her abusive wake-up call. But Hadley didn't scold her boy, only laughed at this daily ritual, in all likelihood promoting a lifetime streak of orneriness in her oldest child. When he was a bit older, he tricked her into thinking lye soap was chocolate as he proffered his mother a seemingly tasty, extravagant treat. Tears sprang to Hadley's eyes as she willed the nasty substance down. No matter, however: PJ knew he had gotten the best of her. Yet again he outfoxed his young mother when he deliberately acted naughty so that she might chase after him to punish her sly little rascal -- who even more calculatedly chose a briar patch to run through, aware that Hadley was scooting after him barefooted).

Even the most diffident female will typically become a mother lioness for her cub, which is exactly what happened to Hadley when she had her son. Now she had someone she cared for more than she cared for Perry... more than she cared for herself... and sure as Hell more than she cared what any one of these townspeople thought. She would be damned if she and her baby were going to sit inside day after day to satisfy someone's moral righteousness! So Hadley took PJ with her everywhere she went - proudly, boldly - and when the weather warmed she set him in a second-hand playpen outside their front yard.

Any sage mother also knows that when caring for an infant or a toddler, the days are often long and tedious, yet the years go by in an instant. Hadley and her little boy were no different; before she knew it PJ was two years old, walking and talking, developing his own *very definite* personality. Perry was a caring family man and a concerned provider, keeping one eye on his variable wife and the other on his fluctuating checkbook. They managed - maybe more than managed - as a little trio, and by the summer of 1934 Hadley was in the family way once more.

Chapter Thirty-One

Felicia Dorothy Wallace was born on April 9th, 1935, and while Perry was pleased as punch to have a little girl now, Hadley felt at odds with her tiny daughter almost from the start. The trouble may have begun with the baby's countenance: practically from birth, she was just TOO exquisite-looking for her tired, frumpy-feeling mother. (Among other abuses to her looks, after carrying two babies in under two-and-a-half years, Hadley thought her belly resembled the sad face of a basset hound and she was repulsed by it). Even more unsettling, her beautiful daughter bore an uncanny resemblance to the late Buddy - but by appearance only! Perry made the mistake of pointing this out to his weary wife - thinking perhaps it would be a comfort to her - and then repeating the observation once too often. He was obviously proud of Felicia's beauty, fond of saying she looked just like a porcelain doll. So he began calling his baby daughter 'Dolly', and the nickname stuck. Dolly was meek and quiet but very, very stubborn... PJ didn't seem to like her any more than Hadley did.

When Dolly's hair grew in it was wavy and auburn-colored -- so thick and lustrous, it rivaled her magnificent face. Perry again put his foot in his mouth by saying he had always had a preference for good-looking redheads; before Dolly was two years old, Hadley marched her down to Donna Dee's for a stern bob. *Aunt Dolly told me how Grandma habitually made her cut her hair, EVERY time it was starting to look long and pretty, that Dolly resented this and could never understand WHY. She said it seemed as though Grandma had a vendetta against beautiful long hair and in fact, she did the same thing with my sisters and me: took us of to get severely short, boyish-looking haircuts - the kind that take YEARS to grow out - without even getting our mother's permission!*

Perry had been a steady father to PJ and a conscientious provider, but he probably took more care of Dolly than he did of his son because she did not get along with her mother. Fortuitously, this man who was so good with numbers found a better job - as a cost accountant - and the growing family moved to a bigger house, on Ellis Street. Just as Perry liked to shower Hadley with gifts whenever he could afford to, so he did the same thing now with Dolly -- and this was likely another point of contention between mother and daughter, not to mention Perry and his son.

As for PJ, he was demonstrating signs of precociousness from an early age: while Dolly was still in diapers, the four-year-old boy began teaching himself how to read. On Sundays he liked to sit on his father's lap at the kitchen table after their breakfast and read him the funnies. Perry was amused by this and not a little impressed; he wanted to show Hadley what their son could do. For some strange reason his wife was upset by this activity - told him the comic strips would 'rot PJ's brain' - and then actually insisted they be banned from their home! It seemed harmless enough to Perry and quite masterly of his son. He never did come to understand what was so offensive to Hadley about some innocuous funny papers -- what it was about them where she clearly could not tolerate the funnies being read and enjoyed in her presence whatsoever.

When my younger sister and I were little girls, our grandma used to bribe us into massaging her neck and shoulders for what seemed like hours at a time. This was in the summer on the dock of our lakeside retreat and she paid us generously for our efforts. We liked to use the money to buy Archie comic books at the drugstore in town -- and Grandma seemed to know this was where we spent our pay. She'd admonish us afterward, saying while of course we could spend any money she gave us however we'd like, '...for Goodness sake, I hope you girls didn't use it on some silly comic books. What a waste!'

Chapter Thirty-Two

Hadley had not received an incriminating letter in a long time. A very long time. She still felt like someone might be watching her, following her around in her automobile and peering inside her windows and it scared her, so she made sure to take extra precautions to keep her family - and the secret of her clandestine affair with Ari - safe. One day her faithful friend Thelma brought over a basket of eggs from her folks' farm that Hadley had specifically requested, planning to share a mid-morning cup of coffee with her chimerical girlfriend. They were both mothers now to young, boisterous children, so mornings for a leisurely cup of coffee together were typically pretty scarce.

She found Hadley in the kitchen of her new home on Ellis Street in the presence of Perry's tool box, apparently trying to lock up their converted ice box. As she watched Hadley struggle with this odd task, Thelma wondered aloud if it was some new-fangled strategy to aid in weight loss -- since she knew her childhood friend struggled with a bit of extra weight around her midriff and still desired to be as slender and attractive as she was back in their high school days, and that securing the ice box perhaps helped to guard against her flagging will power. No, Hadley corrected, she was actually trying to prevent an intruder from poisoning Hadley and her children.

Thelma was incredulous: there WERE no intruders in Liberty and almost no crime -- no one ever locked their doors, not even if they left town, let alone their ice boxes, (it would have been considered rude to do so, not to mention queer), and as far as she was concerned, everyone who lived there was hospitable, trustworthy, and looked out for one another; the citizens of Liberty were good, honest people who had each other's backs. Well, with possibly ONE exception:

Surprisingly, despite the tiny size of their community, Hadley had never come face-to-face with the nefarious Marion Hough since that fateful Sunday Dinner at her ranch so many years ago. It wasn't only that she was a young, harried, middle-class mother of two small children while Marion was a very wealthy, mature widow whose five children were mainly grown -- and they therefore ran on different schedules and in separate circles, with nothing much in common. But since Rufus Hough's passing his wife had been extremely busy overseeing her late husband's various enterprises as well as managing - and let's be honest, meddling - in her five children's lives. All of this frequently took her away from Liberty and sometimes even as far away as Europe, where it was rumored Ari and his wife lived.

But one afternoon in early Fall of '38, Hadley had the unfortunate experience of running smack-dab into the despicable woman in front of the Liberty bandstand with her maid Anna Grunt, who had probably worked for Marion for close to thirty years, and who had no real means of her own. As she got closer, Hadley could see Widow Hough thoroughly haranguing the kind-hearted spinster while balancing an armload of groceries, (no matter what she had to say about Mrs. Hough, Hadley had to admit the woman had always been the very model of efficiency), and this is what she heard:

"Anna, you are such a nincompoop! Are you simply going to stand there and make a hobby out of being useless, or are you going to earn your keep for a change and actually help me with these bags?"

Anna looked downcast and brow-beaten, and Hadley found she just couldn't stand by and without doing SOMETHING. So she marched up, placed herself squarely between the two women, outstretched her long arms in an effort to separate them and declared,

"Back off of her, you miserable old biddy! Why can't you leave this poor woman alone?"

Marion was flabbergasted, but quickly regained her composure. To her recollection, no one - not even her papa - had ever dared speak up to her in entire life -- certainly not in a manner such as this! And she was aware of Dr. Gleeten, Doc

Bachle, Nate Roberts and Harry Wieschmann sitting there on the west side of the bandstand in the late afternoon sun, discussing politics and religion. She appraised her offender, setting a steely gaze upon this evident foe and giving her a Marion-Hough-style-dressing-down with her eyes.

"And who have we here, speaking out of turn, as it seems? Hadley Wallace? Why, YOU, of all people, have no business butting into mine!"

"...You mean the way you butted in between your son and me? Ari wanted to marry me; you knew as much and did whatever you could to prevent it! Mrs. Hough, I daresay it is YOU who are the very embodiment of interference".

The outburst - and its truthfulness - nearly stopped Marion in her tracks. But she quickly recovered.

"I only did what had to be done! What any good mother, who is watching out for the best interests of her son, would do if she were in my shoes. But you would know NOTHING about what a good mother does; now, would you? In fact, you are just like your odd, obscure mother, and that good-for-nothing brother of yours -- only very likely a lot worse!

Why, MRS. Wallace, you sound so dissatisfied with your lot in life. Do you not find your husband satisfactory? Because I - not to mention the rest of Liberty - think he is FAR

TOO GOOD FOR THE LIKES OF YOU! In fact, I've heard it said, many times, that Perry Wallace is a saint or a fool - and probably both!"

Her words were cutting - there was no denying how much they hurt - and Hadley let out a reflexive gasp. More significantly however, this last sentence sounded vaguely familiar to her: she was fairly sure it was at least a paraphrase of one of the final inculpating letters she had received; in fact, as Hadley replayed it in her head, she was certain of it. And this confrontation became the straw that broke the Camel's back for her: the person in their town who seemed to have all the power had once again gotten the best of Hadley, and she had had enough. You could only push a person so far!

So Mrs. Hadley Palmer Wallace pushed Mrs. Marion Hough with all her might, shoving the pernicious woman into some thorny rose bushes surrounding the bandstand -- the very same flower plants that she and Ari had ducked behind whilst planning their rendezvous so many Octobers ago. (Thank Goodness for the thorns).

"Let that be a lesson to you!" Hadley declared, as the older woman struggled, legs flailing and undergarments exposed. She knew she should have stopped there - she had more than made her point - but for some reason Hadley remembered then how Marion had always hated cigar and cigarette smoke, how she had blamed the cigars for her late husband's illness and untimely passing -- and, in particular, how she disapproved of a young lady, (such as Hadley,) smoking with her prized eldest son. And just as a criminal often cannot resist revisiting the scene of his crime, so now Hadley found she just couldn't help herself from hurling one more insult:

"Put THAT in your pipe and smoke it!"

She was sure poor Anna was as surprised as she was, (though probably privately pleased), but didn't dare look at the maid's face, because suddenly she was scared - really, TRULY scared. She rushed off as quickly as she could toward her home on Ellis Street, yet even more than a block away she could still hear the wrath of the one-and-only Marion Hough yelling after her,

"You'll rue the day you ever tried to mess with me, Hadley Wallace!

...rue the day..."

and she felt a fear that went all the way to her groin: THIS was really, TRULY going to be a problem for her.

Yet when she recounted the incident to me nearly sixty years later, my grandma had a bit of a glint in her eye. Even if just for a moment, I could see she had gotten some sweet satisfaction, and I was happy for her triumph.

Chapter Thirty-Three

Thelma was correct: there wasn't any crime to speak of in Liberty, Nebraska back in the 1930's, save for the time during the Depression when a down-and-out father had, out of desperation, stolen some chickens to feed his family. And excluding the annual Halloween pranks of some of the high school boys: soaping store and car windows, upending anything that hadn't been nailed down (their favorite object: tipping over people's outhouses), oh - and one successful bank robbery. Besides this however, there was virtually none. But the town still had a tiny jail, about the size of an outhouse, with steel bars across the front, on the same side of Main Street as Dean's Grocery, set between the State Bank of Liberty and Doc Bachle's office.

And they had a town marshal, or constable, as he was referred to, who had been elected to the position likely by default and was paid for by the 'city'. His name was Raymond Spargur and he was rather dimwitted, still lived with his mother and step-father, and neither drove an automobile nor carried a gun. He never apprehended anyone - Raymond would have been reluctant to do so - and he had a voice that sounded very similar to Mortimer Snerd, one of the puppets made famous by the ventriloquist Edgar Bergen, father of Charlie McCarthy. In fact, unbeknownst to Raymond, the school children called him 'Mortimer' behind his back -- as did many of the adults, truth be told. If you had a problem or needed assistance, you would use your crank telephone to call up Central, who would then try to locate Mortimer, er, Raymond.

This is precisely what Widow Hough had her maid Anna Grunt do that mortifying day in early October 1938 when Hadley Wallace assaulted her in front of the Liberty bandstand. She wanted to exact revenge for herself; she wanted her pound of flesh. When they finally reached Raymond and got him to agree to come downtown, he was thoroughly out of his element in dealing with Marion - as most anyone would be - not to mention that he'd always had a soft spot for the comely Hadley Palmer Wallace.

He stammered and perspired and ultimately refused to lock Hadley up in the unsuitable space, per Widow Hough's request. So the infuriated woman was forced to telephone her lawyer in Wymore, twelve miles away, and place a complaint with the Gage County Seat. This was located at the courthouse over in Beatrice, and Hadley received a summons from the court two weeks after her dubious assault. Incredulous, she read the report a second time as she worried about how to tell Perry. She realized after the fact - and with more than a little irony - that the offense had taken place on October 5th, 1938; the Wallace's seventh wedding anniversary. Oh, Happy Day.

Chapter Thirty-Four

Hadley decided in the end not to say anything to Perry about her Gage County summons; serendipitously, he had to be up in Omaha on business that same day and she was able to leave their children in the capable hands of Thelma and her two lively daughters. She did not even need him for transportation as she had the use of Papa's secondhand truck, now that his deteriorating condition sadly prevented him from driving altogether.

She also had a court-appointed lawyer to defend her from the complaint against her, AND she had her very own self-appointed court attire: an Alice in Wonderland costume. As farfetched as it may sound, Hadley had indeed fashioned together a light blue frock with puffy, oversized sleeves under a crisp white pinafore to wear to the occasion -- reasoning to herself that the summons date was very near Halloween and it made her feel closer to Buddy, who had of course loved the book by Lewis Carroll and especially its central character, not to mention the many times Hadley read the story to her.

As a final touch, she tied a slim black velvet ribbon around her hair. Dolly thought her mama 'looked so pretty' when Hadley bade goodbye to her children that morning; too bad she did not confine the dressing up to playtime with her young daughter, who sorely needed her mother's attention -- and a choice that would have kept Hadley out of even bigger trouble.

This is where her luck ran short, however, because a twister warning had been issued over the radio very early that day, which Hadley unfortunately chose to ignore. She figured it wasn't typical tornado weather, (warm and balmy with a lovely breeze), or the usual time of year, (late spring to mid-summer). In fact, it was quite calm and still - even a bit on the cool side - that morning as she poured herself, and the wide berth of 'Alice's' petticoat into Papa's truck, then drove the twenty-five miles to Beatrice. But the reality is that a tornado can occur anytime, anywhere -- particularly in the Midwest.

The sky had an ominous greenish cast, although perfectly suited to the spirit of Halloween, another indication that a twister was indeed on its way. (The jade color almost always signifies a twister's accompanying and troublesome hailstorm). Then there was the loud and continual rumble, which to her ears sounded like a sinister freight train. When she got to the courthouse Hadley was still mostly all-confidence, though she kept her eyes on the clouds in the sky, scanning its width for an augural funnel shape. When she met with her attorney, Esquire Leroy Dobbs, and noticed his dubious expression as he observed his client was in costume, ('Preposterous!' she thought she heard him say), Hadley felt less certain and for one pregnant moment, she contemplated fleeing court in search of the Green Lantern Inn. In fact, a bit of a bender sounded pretty good to her right about now -- although they might be reluctant to serve her as Alice in Wonderland!

But Mr. Dobbs calmed down and assured her not to worry: the complaint was really nothing serious and any evidence against her was actually quite flimsy. Inside the courtroom Hadley took a seat next to her attorney and to both of their relief, the nasty Mrs. Hough was nowhere to be seen. The judge, a Mr. Marvin White, was emeritus, portly and charitable, and it seemed to Hadley that he took a liking to her right off the bat; she knew she still had a way with most men. Marion Hough's lawyer, Esquire Cecil Cooley, wasn't one of them however, and he liked to do most of the talking -- but it was mostly a lot of hot air. (So the judge said so, much to Mr. Cooley's chagrin).

More portentous rumbling.

Altogether there were only six people in the courtroom, including the judge and the stenographer, but even so, the bailiff still told them to,

"All rise!"

Hadley stood up next to Mr. Dobbs, resplendent in her Alice in Wonderland attire. The judge wondered aloud, albeit cordially, why the respondent was dressed up in costume for a date in his courtroom. He looked over Hadley and the complaint against her - it seemed fairly trivial to him as well - besides, he was all too familiar with the histrionics of the pestilent Mrs. Marion Hough. (He and Mrs. White frequently ran in the same social circles as the Houghs and he himself had never cared for the woman, had actually pitied poor Rufus and speculated that her overbearing nature was what sent him to an early grave, May His Soul Rest in Peace).

The foretelling emerald sky had now turned very, very dark.

And it peeved Judge White that Widow Hough had not set aside time in her own schedule to be present for this hearing if the matter were of such grave importance to her. In truth, he was pretty tempted to dismiss any charges against Mrs. Hadley Wallace and well-aware there had been a tornado warning. In fact, from the courthouse window he could see the prelude to this twister playing out simultaneous to the drama going on inside -- nature's foreshadowing variations seemed to him much like the dramatic vocal commentary of a Greek chorus. First there was lightening, followed by the sound of thunder; then the rain started pouring; next, came a hailstorm, ala the baleful green sky.

But Marion's lawyer was tenacious, verging on insatiable, for her pound of flesh. What a bulldog! He was almost as reprehensible as his client; she had certainly found the perfect mouthpiece for herself in the foul Esquire Cecil Cooley. From Mr. Cooley:

"If it pleases Your Honor, let the court note that the defendant is dressed up as... Alice in Wonderland, is she not? Total and complete buffoonery!" He cried.

"Mrs. Hadley Wallace made a mockery of one Mrs. Marion Hough on the afternoon of October 5th, 1938 when she physically accosted my client beside the Liberty bandstand, which is in the center of Main Street and a popular gathering spot, in front of many respectable citizens of the town, injuring her bodily and causing her mental and physical suffering, as well as anguish because of the public nature of said assault. Which, in point of fact, is wholly unlawful, not to mention disrespectful - and entirely inappropriate! My client requests Your Honor impose the strictest letter of the law and make an example of Mrs. Wallace, lest she think she can somehow get away with this -- and even more troublesome, become a repeat, and potentially more serious, offender.

"Today, it appears the audacious Mrs. Wallace chooses, yet again, to make a mockery of our fine system of justice and to your esteemed Honor by appearing before your Honor as a child would at a playground parade on Halloween. It is just more inappropriate behavior and makes tomfoolery out of our fine system of justice.

Because of this, I urge you to place her in contempt of court". He implored in a *very* loud voice.

The elderly judge had to suppress a chuckle. He cleared his throat, (perhaps to give himself a moment to regain his composure), and asked Hadley to stand before him.

"Mrs. Wallace, while I cannot deny you dress the courtroom up nicely and add a certain festive flair to an otherwise dullard group of men, I need to ask if you mean to mock or incite the ire of the bench?"

"Absolutely not, your Honor." Hadley answered, performing a slight curtsy.

"You do realize this is a serious complaint and Mrs. Hough, in her vexation, calls for the court see justice carried out against you?" the kindly old judge inquired.

"I do, Sir." Another curtsy.

"Well then, Mrs. Wallace, what do you suppose your punishment should be, I wonder?"

Hadley thought for a moment.

"Your Honor, surely you have heard of the childhood saying 'sticks and stones may break my bones, but names will never hurt me'? "

The benevolent judge nodded his ascension.

"But your Honor, I personally find that words can be very hurtful, perhaps even more so than bodily harm.

And there are always two sides to every story, are there not?"

"There are indeed, Mrs. Wallace. And maybe even three - IF you include the purely objective version.

I will allow that you have your own justification for the actions you engaged in on the afternoon of October 5th, 1938. I have no doubt you felt justified and within your right to defend yourself. And I am displeased that the pugnacious Mrs. Hough does not deem it a worthy enough matter to be in the courtroom herself this morning.

At the same time, one cannot take lightly the crime of physical altercation or acting in contempt within the courtroom, both of which you appear to be guilty of. If nothing else, these are irrepressible actions. I, for one, believe the mark of a grown up woman is her ability to repress herself.

I want to meet with both attorneys in my chambers during which time you, Mrs. Wallace, will be detained in a holding room at the basement level of the building. Do you understand what I am saying to you?

Mrs. Wallace?"

Hadley was quiet for a bit, then finally nodded. And curtsied.

"If I choose to release you to your own recognizance after the recess, I trust there will be no further complaints against your character -- specifically by the indignant Mrs. Marion Hough. And no further foolish shenanigans such as dressing up in costume as if you were a child!" The judge reproached her ~ but his tone was merciful.

"Do you think you are a child, Mrs. Wallace?" He asked her gently.

"No, your Honor, I do not. If it pleases the court, Sir, I want you to note that I have two young children of my own and as such, I am all too aware of how actual youngsters behave themselves".

"Then behave yourself as well, Young Lady! It would seem by your actions both on October 5th and again this morning that you need to exhibit far more self-control, Mrs. Wallace".

He was a patient and good-hearted man who did not think for one moment Hadley was a criminal, but he since he had her here before him - and Widow Hough was out for blood - he thought he may as well satisfy the mean old vampire and at the same time teach Hadley a little lesson.

Just then there was a loud, righteous clap of thunder; Mother Nature's admonishment adding to his own, so it seemed.

Judge Marvin White gestured to the bailiff, who took Hadley - aka Alice - down to a holding cell in the basement of the courthouse, an incommodious space (if possible, the room was even smaller than the tiny Liberty jail), with a mere sliver of a window. From her vantage point, Hadley, by straining on the tips of her toes, could see just a fraction of the street above her and viewed debris, with a mixture of leaves, swirling around -- and it felt to her as if the malefic wind was pushing at the courthouse building, despite its considerable size. She could also tell the sky had become very, very dark - nearly pitch black now, even though it was not yet noon. But what she needed was to be able to watch the clouds, so that she might search for a telltale funnel shape. She could not observe the burgeoning weather and even worse, there was no clock, and because of her costume brainstorm, Hadley had decided not to wear her watch that day.

Terrified by the continual menacing rumble, Hadley's imagination and subsequent fear began to get the best of her as she waited and waited and WAITED for someone to please, come release her! She was desperate to get out of that building and home to the safety of her children. She flailed and shouted and wrestled with the door, using both hands to jiggle at the knob, after a while flinging herself into it, shoulder first, and finally banging against it with all her might. She did this over and over - and over - again, until she had torn off one of the puffy shoulders from the costume, badly bruised her left elbow and lost the hair ribbon, just from sheer exertion, and as the time stretched on and on, Hadley thought she might go mad from fear and anxiety.

I believe the powerful force of wind and maelstrom that afternoon when she was held captive are metaphors for my grandmother's psyche and, regrettably, something sort of shifted in her from that day forward.

Unfortunately for Hadley the tornado gathered its strength over the court recess and no one was allowed back into the part of the building where she'd been detained until the uproar had subsided. This restrained, unrestrained woman was all but forgotten as court officials and the bailiff waited out the calamitous twister in a designated area at the opposite end of the courthouse basement. Perhaps she would have had better luck if Hadley had dressed up as Dorothy from The Wonderful Wizard of Oz. At the very least, it would have been more befitting the occasion.

Chapter Thirty-Five

1939: Dolly was four years old now; PJ nearly seven. Even though they were still very young, they knew fairly well what to expect from their mother. Hadley doted on her son and didn't like her daughter much. She was fond of bringing PJ along with her to Lou Lu's for an afternoon beer and cigarette, and sometimes as far away as Beatrice to the Green Lantern Inn -- and one time, a spontaneous trip for just the two of them, without so much as a nod to her husband, to visit Aunt Della in the rocky mountains of Colorado. She'd permit her son to mostly do whatever he wanted, but would either ignore or worse, smother and pester her demure little girl. She didn't like to clean and especially didn't like to cook, so was given to hiring a cleaning woman, (something Perry struggled to afford), and sending her offspring out with empty bellies or convincing them to walk to the drugstore, unescorted, for their noon meal.

They could sense there was a vacillating pattern to life at home with her: Hadley's moods and stamina swung between a saturnine temperament to a frenzy of energy and ideas; her weight would fluctuate by twenty-five pounds or so in either direction, (a technique she'd picked up from her former roommate at the sanitarium: the poor woman virtually starved herself to get her philandering husband's attention, all to no avail) and correlated with the ups and downs of Hadley's disposition. When she was subdued, she also was heavier, though much better groomed; when she acted uninhibited, she became skinny and didn't look - and often smell - so good.

Her hobbies included chain-smoking - a nasty habit PJ in particular deplored and one which wasn't doing any favors for her looks - drinking, often to excess, just like her older brother, and possibly reading IF she could settle down long enough. When overexcited, she slept and ate very little and went from a taciturn demeanor to telephoning everyone in her book -- even by long-distance and at all hours, despite the inconvenience or the cost. In her whirlwind, she'd become passionate about finding assistance for her father, whose arthritis was sadly worse than ever, and liked to have "pow-wows", (meetings with PJ and Dolly, and better yet, the neighborhood children as well, where she would galvanize her troops and dole out an assigned task to each or a group mission). The youngsters could feel when this was coming - much like the way an animal can sense a storm - and did their best to avoid 'the silly lady', scattering like autumn leaves.

Perry remained even-keeled and tried to balance things out as best as he could. And once again, he could see the need to make things fair and square in their home on Ellis Street. For

PJ's fifth birthday nearly two years prior, animal-lover Perry had gotten his son a beagle of his very own, whom PJ named "Skippy". As a boy, Perry had always had a flock of animals to care for, loved this, and wanted the same environment for his children. His namesake quickly, eagerly, learned to train and care for the cute little pup, and the two of them went everywhere together: constant companions.

Yet here was Dolly without much company of her own, save for a disapproving mother, an ailing, arthritic grandpa and a deaf and dreary grandmother. She could use a bit of love and companionship as well -- and as far as Hadley was concerned, a bit of responsibility.

So one evening Perry came home with a darling white puppy, which he - and mostly Dolly - named "Cuddles". Cuddles was irresistible and meant the world to Dolly. For the first time in her life, the somber child was smiling from ear-to-ear. Everywhere Dolly went, so did Cuddles; she whispered her innermost secrets to Cuddles, taught her to do pleasing tricks such as "Sit up, pretty!", and even slept with her fluffy little dog. Perry was privately pleased with himself that he'd managed to find another solution to even up the tally at home and was able to turn the focus back to his job as a cost accountant.

Unfortunately for Dolly and Cuddles - and for no apparent reason - Hadley despised the little dog almost from the start. It was probably more to do with the pushing-Marion-Hough-debacle and subsequent terrifying bedlam than any single thing about the animal itself: the person she perceived to have all the power had gotten the best of her one too many times, she had been traumatized by her courthouse confinement, and she was beginning to lash out now -- particularly if she perceived weakness in another.

One fine Saturday while PJ and Dolly were at the circus with their Aunt Lucille, who'd come to town for a brief visit, poor Cuddles got stuck inside the house with only Hadley to rely upon. It was a beautiful early summer day and she was desperate to get outside, relieve herself, and meet up with her pal Skippy. Cuddles tried to get Hadley's attention by placing herself in front of the strange lady, finding her gaze and cocking her head to the side. Irresistible to most people - but not to Hadley. When this didn't work she started whimpering, eventually crying - finally howling - all to no avail. Hadley sat in her chair in that parlor room, rocking back and forth,

baaaaack and fooorrrtth,

staring at the pitiful pup, taunting her with frightening expressions and tormenting Cuddles by mocking her pleas. This went on for quite a while before Hadley got down

off her rocker

and onto her knees, mimicking the little dog's stance and pretending she was a canine as well: scratching, sniffing - even barking at her - snarling, and foaming at the mouth, the spittle dribbling down her chin and onto the rug. Who can say how long the two went round and round like this until, ultimately, the stand-off was just too much for Cuddles and she simply couldn't take it anymore. So she surrendered to the cruel mistress, gave up her innocent little canine plans, tucked her tail between her legs and scampered out of the room, piddling away in defeat, desperation... and shame.

Chapter Thirty-Six

Life went on this way, more or less, for the next few years, in spite of Hadley's ups and downs. By 1942 World War II had involved the United States and rightfully impacted the good citizens of Liberty: they kept patriotic candles burning in their windows, respectfully abided the rationing of meat, (*'unless you raised your own livestock'*), and gasoline. The Wallace family made similar sacrifices, such as walking everywhere they possibly could throughout the year so that they might save up their allotment to take their annual summer car trip to Minnesota, and each week the high school sold savings bonds and war stamps.

PJ took a near-obsessive interest in tracking the war and made a huge display on his bedroom wall. He turned beans into soldiers to better re-enact their battles, admonishing his mother to leave his bedroom undisturbed of all wartime clutter, and waited eagerly along with the rest of the town for updates in the monthly Liberty Bell News. Most of all PJ and the other townspeople were keenly aware of the boys who had to go off to fight the good fight. *"You knew the boys that had to go", Grandma told me, "and it made you ache for them and their families".* The photographs of the fallen were displayed prominently in the box office window of The

Comet. Regrettably, the barber's eldest and profoundly handsome son Edward, as well as Ari's light-hearted younger brother Beauly, were among the war's latest victims.

Hadley's children were both in school now full-time while Papa had settled into a nursing home -- his arthritis so debilitating, he just couldn't manage by himself anymore. Bertha came to live with Hadley and her little family in their house on Ellis Street, but it didn't last for very long. One day when she arrived home with a sack of groceries, Hadley discovered her mother flailing about on the kitchen floor. Apparently Bertha had once again attempted to take her own life -- on this occasion, by jumping from the top of the family's new Frigidaire. What the Hell? Lord only knows how such a large, unwieldy woman ever managed to get up to the top of the refrigerator to begin with!

It was always the same with her mama: Bertha's actions engendered far more questions than answers. And of course, she still refused to talk -- so it was a moot point asking her anything to begin with. This surely would have traumatized Hadley's youngsters, had they been the ones to find their grandmother, and God forbid she'd been successful. It was also more than her middle daughter could manage and thus necessitated a telephone call from Perry to Hadley's Aunt Johnnie, (the oldest sister of Bertha and Della), who agreed to come and collect her miserable, misunderstood sibling and move her in with Johnnie and her husband, several hours drive away.

Incredibly, and so very tragically, not long after this the Palmers were struck with the horrific news that fire had claimed yet another member of their long-suffering family: Lucille had met and married a fellow while working as a secretary at a pharmaceutical company in Chicago, and one day an alcohol vat caught fire, killing several employees; Lucille's tall new husband among them. And just as Perry had called on Aunt Johnnie to come and rescue her sister, so now did Lucille ask for Hadley. Despite their differences Hadley went to her widowed sister at once, leaving both children and their pets in the care of their father for an indeterminate stay. Ever-patient an unassuming, he did not press his wife on the matter of when she'd be coming home to them. Perry - and PJ and Dolly - did not see Hadley again for nearly a year.

I tried my best to coax Grandma into telling me about this year away from her family, but it was obvious she just wasn't comfortable talking about it. When I asked my Dad, he said he remembered that one morning his mother gave him and his sister a perfunctory hug and a kiss and some Lunch money - yet they did not see her again until after they had been promoted to the next grade! Otherwise, he was pretty tight-lipped on the matter as well.

... Though later on he did share how his father finally located his wayward wife in a state sanitarium in southern California -- and that Hadley was subsequently sent by Perry back to Chicago, this time for an abortion.

Chapter Thirty-Seven

My dad was never told about Buddy's fiery death when he was growing up - let alone that there even WAS a Buddy - at least not from his mother. But he still found out Hadley had a younger sister who would have been his aunt, but had been tragically killed when she was roughly the same age he was now - nearly thirteen - and unfortunately for PJ, he had to learn about it in an equal parts fiendish and terrifying way. (*Why is it kids can be so cruel? I swear, this is one of life's biggest mysteries - and school children in particular are often the worst offenders).* By the time he was twelve–and-three-quarters, it had been long enough since her explosive death by house fire for the tragedy to become morbid playground folklore, and fodder for the other children to tease and taunt him over -- to bait, bandy and even bully him a bit because of his association with her.

Since he was utterly oblivious to the aunt who had died when she wasn't much older than he was now, PJ likewise did not know about the small woebegone grave in the Liberty cemetery with its sepulchral little headstone:

Florence Jean Palmer

Beloved Daughter and Sister

1918 - 1931

It beheld a tiny oval-shaped picture of Buddy, her final school portrait, and was donated by the shady (read: greedy and very likely culpable) store that had sold her the hazardous - but cheaper - gasoline in place of the more costly kerosene she had actually paid for. Now it was nearing Halloween again, not to mention PJ's thirteenth birthday and his schoolmates made up the perfect game by which to arouse the diabolical mood of the season, and of course terrorize the adolescent boy - and naturally his naïve younger sister Dolly.

In fairness to his classmates, it all began somewhat organically when an unusually violent electrical storm made its wrathful path through Liberty just days before one of the children's favorite holidays with a force of wind formidable enough to blow the roof from the Hough's large henhouse -- and all the feathers off their hens and roosters! Liberty High School, which had been built in the mid-1800's and had at the top of its roof a dark, inauspicious wooden cupola, would not come out of it unscathed either. Unlike most cupolas, this one did not have an accompanying - and oh-so-necessary, particularly if built in the Midwest - vertical lightning rod. One especially angry bolt had struck the roof and taken it off and as a consequence, made what remained of the building look quite different from its original form, and unfortunately for the boys and girls, not nearly as menacing -- certainly not eerie enough to set the tone for this most frightening of occasions.

They therefore felt the need to drum up some ghoulish morale; being allowed the day of Halloween to climb from a ladder and down into their classroom windows dressed in costume was not very satisfying, especially for the older children. The boys in particular were on the prowl for something more spine-chilling with which to occupy their vigorous imaginations.

So one day after school toward the very end of October when they had been playing six-man football and PJ needed to call a time out due to a sprained finger and thus had gone off in search of John Hart for a bit of first aid, the boys no longer had enough players for their game and set about playing a half-hearted round of hide-and-go-seek instead. They disappeared all over the school grounds: into the large outhouse even after their principal, Miss Hinman, admonished from her office window, "Do not go in there!"; under some of the various wooden seats tethered to the large May pole at the center of the playground; beneath the benches in the gymnasium, and even on the fire escape staircase. In fact, Dwayne Fisher was bold enough to slide down the round metal fire slide, despite knowing full-well that this was strictly forbidden, except on the last day of school, the day the children were given their final report cards, a picnic dinner with their families and had free run of the place. When they'd lost interest in the game and PJ still had not returned, the boys began to talk about the uncanny Buddy and speculate how she might just haunt the grounds now and again, if only they could find a way to conjure her spirit from the grave. But *how* to arouse her essence? They wondered.

While the charitable Mr. Johnny took his time tending to the lad, PJ's classmates tried unsuccessfully to have a bit of a séance right there on the field, yet it was no good. The day was pleasant and boring, and ultimately they figured they needed PJ - and probably Dolly as well - to incite Buddy's ghost. Oh, well. Maybe they should just head over to the cemetery and have a look at her grave, Dwayne suggested. This peaked their interest and as luck would have it, here came PJ at last -- with Dolly dutifully tagging along a few steps behind him. And thus a game began that was anything but playful - or childish.

"Hey, PJ!" Dwayne called out. "Wanna find yer burned up Aunt Buddy?" What PJ wanted, desperately, was to be accepted by his peers, so at first he was intrigued, but then quickly perplexed, and Dwayne and the other boys picked up on his confusion.

"What's a matter, PJ?" Jerry Andrews asked him. "Don'tcha know about your charbroiled Aunt Buddy?"

"I don't have an 'Aunt Buddy'!" PJ retorted. "I have an Aunt Lucille, who's RICH, who lives in Chicago, I think, and I have a Great Aunt Della who's even richer, who lives in the Rocky Moun-"

"Of course you have an Aunt Buddy! Just ask your mother if you don't believe me. You have an aunt and she's a ghost, 'cept her face and hands is all burned up, and she's black as TAR!" Jerry shouted as the others started snickering, then chanting,

"Black as tar. Black as tar. PJ has an aunt and she's black as tar!"

"... In fact, we was just lookin' fer her" Dwayne added. "Maybe you and your snot-nosed sister can help us!"

Dolly was wide-eyed and speechless and latched on to PJ's hand. Now, normally her older brother would not have been caught dead holding hands with his sister, let alone out in public - and PARTICULARLY in front of his peers but he was getting the creeps pretty hard and fast here, and PJ found he just couldn't help himself. (Besides, his other hand was throbbing from the football injury; Mr. Johnny had been overzealous, wrapping his fingers much too tightly). Dwayne and Jerry became the ring-leaders then and proceeded to guide PJ and Dolly and the other children back through the maze of their hide-and-seek game, calling out:

"Is Buddy in the outhouse?"

"*Na! She isn't in the outhouse...*" they sang.

"Is Buddy in the gymnasium, under the benches?" they asked, all lightness and innocence.

"*Na, she isn't in the gymnasium and she ain't under the benches...*" went their chorus,

"Is Buddy on the May pole?" they cooed, (Dolly's favorite place to play),

"*Na, she ain't on the May pole...*"

...and so on until they had exhausted all of their schoolground hiding places. The game was beginning to lose steam. PJ had proclaimed it 'Stupid' and the day was suddenly getting late, when one of the other boys had another inspiration:

"Hey, I know where she is", Barney Lowe interrupted, "the CEMETERY!"

"*Let's go!*" the others cried.

By this time PJ was agitated, feeling the pain from his football injury and anxious to be home -- he knew his mother would be worrying about why her children were not yet back from school.

But he couldn't risk the fellows finding out he was afraid and besides, curiosity ate the cat: he really did want to know if he did, in fact, have an Aunt Buddy... and what had happened to her. So he followed the other boys, dragging his sister along with him, the three-quarters of a mile walk down the highway. The Liberty Cemetery, established early in the 1800's, was even older than the school, wrought iron fenced and well-tended, save for some autumn leaves swirling about its lugubrious graves. The gang of boys were very pleased with themselves when they'd at last revealed Buddy's forlorn little plot to PJ and his dovelike sister.

PJ just stood there, staring at Buddy's portrait - while she seemed to stare back at him - and couldn't get over her resemblance to Dolly, except for the color of her hair, and he was unnerved by her nearness in age to himself. He was mesmerized to be making her acquaintance, such as it was, overcome by emotion, yet all of a sudden infuriated with his mother for never telling him about her younger sister and their family legacy of tragedy. The boys seemed to have faded into the background for a bit -- until Dwayne sidled up to PJ and whispered in his ear,

"Ya know, your aunt was kinda pretty before her face was burned off and both her hands and all her fingers!"

Then he and Jerry - and finally the others - started throwing rocks at her tombstone, crying out,

"Wake up, Buddy! WAKE UP, BUDDY! Come on out! We know you're in there!!"

"Yeah, we know you're in there, and we're not afraid!" Dwayne goaded.

Now they were tormenting her sacred space with rocks, defiling the sanctity of this reunion and Buddy's uncorrupted memory, and PJ felt a hatred swell from deep inside of him.

"STOP IT!!" he raged and held back a fist. Though he had an injured hand, (it was his left hand, the one he favored), and he was a slight boy, short like his father - and certainly no fighter - PJ felt a fury boiling inside himself that would have taken out the best of them. Dolly sensed as much and in a wisdom beyond her years, as well as a rare and lifelong sensitivity, she tugged at her brother's sleeve and pulled him away from the melee; the younger one leading the older. *My Aunt Dolly was unworldly, as her late aunt had been before she became other-worldly.* Only after the two of them were safely through the cemetery gates did they begin to run, running like the wind then along the rural route and into pitch blackness, running home for safety - and answers.

Hadley had indeed been worried about her youngsters. It was nightfall with no sign of either one of them and Perry unavailable, off at The Comet on the second floor of the old theatre for an Eastern Star meeting. She couldn't imagine what they could be up to and her mind had gone into overdrive with all sorts of unspeakable scenarios. When they finally burst through the front door, bright-eyed and breathless, she noticed PJ had a bandaged hand, yet was undeterred in her fury with the two of them - but likewise PJ was enraged with his mother - and he confronted her before she could him:

"Mother, you're a liar!" he accused.

"Where have you two been?" she demanded. "Answer me!

I have a mind to give you both a sound licking! Just wait until I tell your father about this!" she warned.

"Don't threaten me, Mother!" PJ retorted. "And don't lie to me, either. I've just come from the cemetery - so has Dolly - and I've seen Buddy's gravestone with my own two eyes. I saw her picture, too - she looks just like Dolly - and I know she was my same age when she died.

...Why didn't you tell me I had an aunt who burned to death in a fire when she was only thirteen years old?" PJ demanded.

"What are you talking about?!" Hadley cried.

"WHY didn't you ever tell us about her?" PJ repeated. "You made me look like such an idiot!"

he accused. PJ was bright and emboldened, and he wasn't backing down.

Hadley did not answer her son's questions. Instead, she grabbed her purse and a set of car keys and bolted from their home on Ellis Street, leaving her children in the entry way - cold, confused, hungry - and most of all, frightened.

The Chevrolet was later found abandoned in the parking lot at Beatrice's Green Lantern Inn, Hadley nowhere in sight. She missed Halloween, and thus her son's thirteenth birthday; she missed a lot of things. And though she was not gone for an entire year this time, she was away long enough to necessitate another trip to Chicago - for another abortion.

She never had asked PJ about his injured hand.

Chapter Thirty-Eight

Perry knew, in his heart, that his family could not go on this way any longer. He had already lost his only sibling Albertus to a fatal heart attack before the man was even thirty-three years old. His older brother had rheumatic fever when he was a boy and it may very well have weakened his heart -- but so had Perry begun experiencing recurrent and, at times, very sharp chest pains. He had taken to walking everywhere including a regular midday jaunt around town on his noon lunch hour, given up the Lucky Strike cigarettes, and found God, (by age forty-six, the year of his first heart attack, he began to go to church in earnest, attending services nearly every week). And he tried his best to ignore Hadley's obvious - and of course terribly hurtful and embarrassing - marital indiscretions. On her good days, she still had a bit of spunk and moxie, but those times were becoming fewer and further between, and no matter how hard Perry tried to control his own habits and behaviors, these efforts would never be enough to change his capricious wife.

Most recently he had come home from a long, exhaustive day at his office to discover Hadley had arranged for the sale of their family's prized piano with no logical reason for this action whatsoever. Not only had it required years for him to set aside enough money for its purchase, Dolly had been taking weekly lessons in their home since she was five, becoming quite the accomplished little pianist, and it was one of the few things in her life that brought his daughter real joy.

He had kept the promise he'd made to himself on that evening in the park so many years ago when a young Hadley had enthralled him, unwittingly tugging at his heartstrings - now his daughter's piano strings - yet it had come at such a cost, all the harder to overlook when one is an accountant and he could see it was creating an enormous debt for his children, *particularly* Dolly. They were fortunate to have means and a nice home but it remained unstable, and both their budget and household were slaves to Hadley's unpredictable whims and activities. It was time for her husband to step up and take action, or ultimately they would all go down with the sinking ship, the SS Hadley. Herbert was the sailor in the family, not his sister -- and certainly neither Perry nor the children, for that matter.

He honestly did not know what else to do; he was an accountant, after all, one who used the double-entry method daily. At work Perry needed his assets and liabilities to be in perfect balance by the end of each day -- and yet the life he'd made at home with Hadley was so terribly out of whack. So, after carefully tallying his personal checks and balances he decided to look up Dr.

Paul Prentiss - who still had a practice and sanitarium in Wichita - and when he got the doctor on the telephone, explained what he was dealing with -- including the squirm-worthy confession of her blatant promiscuity. (For some time now Bell Telephone had been going around from little town to little town, paying households two hundred dollars apiece for their old crank telephones and replacing these independent systems with black, desk-type telephones that, thankfully, could be used to make private calls). Discretion was the better part of valor -- and in this case, an absolute imperative.

In addition to Hadley's unaccounted times away from her family, Perry was aware that his wife still liked to go to Lou Lu's in the afternoons while his children were in school and she was often alternately accompanied by two no-account men, Clay Collier and Phil Coburn. Perry was not fleecable to their intentions; it had been years now, if ever, since he could trust his headstrong wife.

Dr. Prentiss remembered the young, tormented bride and was intrigued by what Perry described to him over the telephone.

"It sounds as though Mrs. Wallace may very well suffer from a mental condition known as manic depression", he told her concerned husband. "The extreme variations in mood and temperament you describe, her voracious appetite - be it for food or sexual in nature - her impulsive and destructive behavior, and the harsh reality that you and your children cannot rely upon Hadley to be stable, secure presence in your home all suggest this psychological malady.

I encourage you to bring your wife back to Prentiss for further evaluation. We have far better treatment for the mentally ill than we did before - ways to actually inflict controlled damage to a patient's brain - as well as medication that was unavailable when she was a patient here so many years ago.

There is something new and quite exciting you may have heard about that originated in Italy: electroconvulsive therapy, or 'electric shock treatment'. It is useful in suppressing a patient's nervous system and we use it to treat major depressive disorders such as you describe in your wife. We can often produce a complete, positive change in psychoses; I assure you, Mr. Wallace, its efficacy is really quite high.

As I recall Mrs. Wallace experienced a terrible emotional loss prior to coming here previously and this therapy has good success at destroying past unfavorable memories, which likely triggered both her deep depression and perhaps her more distressing - and certainly far more destructive - mania".

Perry listened very carefully to every word the doctor said and felt certain by the end of their conversation that Paul Prentiss was indeed describing his wife -- and maybe, just maybe, a way out of this nightmare. For the first time in a very long time, Perry was hopeful. And then he felt it: another cryptic chest pain... or was it? Maybe it was actually relief he sensed, an emotion which had evaded him for many, many years now.

Chapter Thirty-Nine

When Dr. Paul Prentiss finally laid eyes on Mrs. Hadley Wallace, he could see straight away that she was a far different woman from the young bride he had treated more than a decade-and-a-half ago. Gone was the gorgeous, if tragic, young woman with a slender yet beautifully voluptuous form, creamy skin and natural glow of beauty and youth. In her place was a dejected, somewhat overweight matron with a dull complexion, dry hair and lifeless eyes. Everything seemed to sag about Hadley now, from her spirits to her posture to her bosom. He could see a ragged scar over her left eyebrow; he could see that time had not been her friend. Mrs. Wallace had endured -- but still she did not have much to live for. Dr. Prentiss hoped on this occasion he could really help. And he was rooting most of all for Perry and their children.

He began with an interview, just Hadley and himself, and took careful inventory of her accounting of the years since she'd last been his patient. He asked about her melancholy. He delved into her bursts of hyperactivity. He encouraged her to confide in him the depth of the hostility she felt toward her young daughter and even pressed her to explore her flights from home, not to mention Hadley's various, sundry extramarital activities.

He made it clear throughout the process he did not judge Mrs. Wallace, he only desired to help and restore peace of mind to both herself and her family. She would be treated, he decided after all, with Cardiazol therapy -- though truth be told, it was somewhat against her will. And so when the interview between Dr. Paul Prentiss and his wife was completed and her husband had been conferred upon, the metal doors shut before him and Perry could hear Hadley being wheeled down the hospital corridor on a slim gurney, an intermittent 'squeak' of a rubber wheel against the sanitarium floor, as one was a bit loose.

When Hadley had electric shock treatment, it was absolutely terrifying for her; *'The therapy felt like a fire which had spread throughout my body. My brain was fairly trembling'.* She later wrote Lucille in a rare stroke of confession.

Sadly, she would endure this form of 'therapy' three more times in her life -- the final episode just days before my parent's wedding when she was at a bridal luncheon for my mother and thought she was in the company of Paul Revere, ranting of his midnight ride while pacing the hostess' living room, her beloved cat, Mishke, in her arms.

She was thereafter prescribed Lithium to stabilize her mood swings, which Perry made sure to watch her take since, at the first hint she was feeling better, she believed she no longer required medication - *of course.* He thought it best - and frankly necessary - to give their family a fresh start, (he'd heard the gossip; he knew the school children liked to call her 'Madly Hadley'), and so the four of them and their pets moved from Liberty to Beatrice to get away from the incessant whisperings and the glare of speculation -- to give PJ, and especially Dolly, a fighting chance.

Perry spent every free moment he had with Hadley from that point on: helping nurture their teenage children, taking his wife for long country drives, to movies, shows and out to dinner, and always, summer vacations in their beloved Minnesota. He now made a wonderful salary as a senior cost accountant, (over ten thousand dollars annually), had saved and invested wisely – thanks in large part to Aunt Della, whose idea of going to market was the *stock* market - and as such, they could afford quite a lot: new cars for their children, fine college educations, all the household help Hadley needed or desired, a fancy wedding for Dolly -- and an island on Lake Burntside - 'Felicia's Island' - that was named for and given to his beautiful daughter.

Upon his retirement in early 1965, Perry bought himself and his bride a peaceful lakeside retreat back where they had known their first - and maybe only genuine - happiness together, back in the northern woods of Minnesota.

Chapter Forty

The grand plan? To spend every May through October at their private cabin and retreat on the remote, heavily wooded Lake Vermilion. Hadley now had Perry's constant focus and companionship; their children both married to good, steady mates and building lives and families of their own, far from Nebraska, and far from the scepter of Hadley's mental illness.

The couple spent that spring buying sturdy secondhand items to furnish the place, carefully selecting a fishing boat with an outboard motor, a canoe, and paddleboat for their young grandchildren -- setting up this retirement compound to their personal satisfaction.

They unloaded Hadley's favorite books and her husband's fishing rods and tools; Perry, it seemed, would be able to live out his lifelong dream of a Minnesota lake house of his very own. He and Hadley liked to fish in the mornings, paddle around in their canoe or nap in the afternoons and play cards and visit with their hospitable lakeside neighbors in the evenings.

Sometimes they drove into Cook, the nearest town, and had a beer and a smoke, (at least for Hadley,) at a local tavern, Old Muni, or over to The Crescent for trout supper and a bit of dancing. Perry loved a robust thunder storm, and there were plenty to satisfy his hunger for them. He could sit inside the cabin at the kitchen table with a cup of coffee and watch the entire thing unfurl itself across the lake.

On mild nights they often brought two plaid fold-out chairs down to the dock to watch the sun as it was setting. The water was a virtual mirror of the northern sky - so far north and so beautiful that it did seem closer to God - and they could see firsthand then why the lake was called 'vermilion'. The evening mating call of the loons was their personal lullaby, a prelude to a good night's sleep, and the sweet scent of ripening berries pervaded the atmosphere.

The only things that dampened their spirits were the pesky mosquitos which by June were a constant presence and nuisance, ('Minnesota's unofficial state bird' Perry joked, and Hadley agreed), and his sporadic, troublesome chest pains. Mostly they anticipated July when my father, now a chemistry professor of some renown, and his wife would drive up from the South with their three little girls for an extended family vacation.

Sadly, this good-hearted grandfather's heart wasn't so good anymore after all and he wasn't at the lake to greet PJ and his brood when they arrived. Instead, Perry suffered his second heart attack the day before their reunion would have taken place and was taken by ambulance to the closest hospital in tiny nearby Cook. My parents went to visit as soon as they had heard the awful news, and lifted their infant daughter - me - up outside his hospital room window so that Grandpa Perry might have a better look at his newest grandchild. He smiled and waved at me and blew airy kisses; Mother promised him she would put me in his arms just as soon as he was stronger.

But he never did get to hold me - never got out of there alive - and did not have his golden years in 'God's Country'. Instead, Perry George Wallace had his third - *things always come in threes* - and this time, fatal, heart attack on the Fourth of July, 1965, and his body was taken by train back to Nebraska, accompanied by PJ and Hadley, and joined thereafter by Dolly, for his burial in Omaha alongside his father, mother and older brother.

It should have been a hero's.

PART THREE

"We are all miracles

wrapped up in chemicals"

from the song Wonderful, by Gary Go

Chapter Forty-One

My relationship with my paternal grandmother, Harriet Della Palmer Wallace, got off to a dubious start - or *non*-start - and truthfully, it never gathered much steam thereafter. In May of 1964 my mother's mother Thelma, the very same, often long-suffering - and sometimes only friend of Hadley's, took a tumble on a sidewalk, badly bruising her left knee, when she was walking door-to-door through Liberty, soliciting donations for the American Cancer Society. My mother Shirley was Thelma's oldest daughter and as a little girl, a frequent childhood playmate of my dad's. They lost touch after Dad's family moved to Beatrice. The pair were later reunited during a chance train ride into Lincoln when they were both attending the University of Nebraska.

Thelma had taken a fall three years earlier while she was visiting Washington DC but at the time she had been anxious to get right back to Liberty for the harvest, so ignored her injuries; when Thelma finally went to Doc Bachle, he 'gave her heck' for not seeking earlier medical treatment.

"You could have gotten blood clots!" He admonished her.

So this time around, Thelma did everything right: she went to her doctor straight away, was admitted to the hospital, kept on strict bed rest and monitored closely. But what should have been a routine visit to treat her for the risk of *possible* blood clots turned out to be her fateful stay, (Thelma's last words to her nurse: *"I feel like I am floating away"*), and she died within the hour. It was the Friday afternoon before Mother's Day weekend in early May. She knew by then that Mom was going to be a mother again herself - and after two little girls she said she hoped I'd be a boy and that I'd be my Mom's last baby. Even though Shirley was only a few months along, Thelma had already planned to come South for my birth and its aftermath.

Grandma was well-aware of this as well: fellow mothers-in-law and still close friends at the time of Thelma's accidental fall, she and Perry were actually on their way to Lincoln to visit her but when they arrived, Thelma was gone, her bed already cool, her hospital room empty. She felt badly for her late friend and was awfully fond of Shirley, so Grandma offered - insisted, really - that when my birth was imminent she would be there to help look after us all. She was eager to do a good job on behalf of Thelma and very much up for the task; her only daughter Dolly had two children of her own by this time -- yet hadn't wanted her mother there for either of their births. Grandpa Perry recognized the sanctity of this privilege and thanked my mom profusely. Thanked her, but as the gatekeeper of Grandma's medicine and her stability, he worried too.

Now punctuality has never been my strong suit - my birth was no exception - and so my due date, October 23rd, 1964 came and went without so much as a rumble. By Halloween - Dad's 32nd Birthday - Mom was eight days late, becoming anxious and uncomfortable, so she trick-or-treated well into the night with my older sisters, hoping to get things going and get me out of there. Eviction time! Her girls were game for the adventure and the chance to stay up well after their bedtime -- the younger of the two so little she was 'trick-or-riding' in a stroller... Still nothing.

On Friday evening, November 6th, I was finally ready to make my appearance yet Dad, true to form himself, made some off-hand comment Grandma took offense to and she abruptly packed her things and left by train for Beatrice, so consequently she never made my acquaintance, never helped my poor mother - who was overwhelmed by now and sorely missing Thelma - and 1964 ended without any personal fanfare for either one of us.

When Perry passed away the following July, Grandma flew back to Lake Vermilion after his funeral with Dad and promptly gave the cabin, boats, furniture and all other accoutrements to my father. There was a black-and-white photograph taken - the only one that's just the two of us and so by omission, my favorite - of Grandma and myself perched on the dock. I am eight months old, grinning from ear-to-ear, as Grandma holds and appears to be tickling me, seducing me. I like to think I inherited those same smiling eyes and that hopefully I brought some comfort to a grieving new widow as only a sweetly soft and snuggly baby can do. This is most likely as close or affectionate as we ever were for many years to come.

Chapter Forty-Two

By the time I was three years old our family had settled in northern California, where my father accepted a tenured faculty position at a prestigious university. I was a big sister now; there were four little girls and our family was complete. Grandma came to visit us in sunny California for the holidays. Mom was busy in the kitchen juggling a colicky baby and a pot roast when she overheard my sister Kate, who was five years old at the time, say to Grandma - plain as day -

"No one else likes you - but I do".

Out of the mouth of babes, right? The words hung there in the air and Mom 'just about died from embarrassment', yet the sentiment was true and none of us bothered to correct her. Grandma wasn't mean, she wasn't fearsome, she was... *off-putting.* Kate seemed to be on a similar wave length however and the two of them shared an undeniable connection -- though Grandma was equally good to all of us, much to her credit. She liked to 'salt and pepper' our arms and then pretend she was munching up and down them as if our arms were chicken legs; she loved fried chicken. She liked to indulge us in clothing stores she called 'Grandma Traps' and she conducted pow-wows with another hapless generation. I recall one of my missions was to make sure to turn out every light in a room before I left it; I *still* get a little anxious about a light being left on if a room is empty. Financially speaking she was incredibly generous, routinely giving each of her four granddaughters large birthday and Christmas checks and a thousand dollars for every one of our graduations. It seemed like a lot of money at the time. It was. She even paid for my oldest sister's law school education and while we were yet little girls she would pull us aside, one at a time, and say, conspiratorially that she'd give us a thousand dollars if we eloped like she and Perry had, instead of having a costly wedding.

She was a contradiction of extravagance and simplicity. Known for wearing her fur coat and an enormous diamond bauble everywhere, she ate simply, cheaply, twice a day, every day, at her local hospital cafeteria. She still loathed to cook. She bought herself a different car every single year, yet they were typically inexpensive models. Always faithful to Fords, their Pintos became her signature choice when she got older. I'm pretty sure her only new dresses were the ones my Mom bought her for her birthday.

I wanted a 'normal' grandmother in the worst possible way. I'd lament to my mom on too many occasions that I wished it had been Thelma who'd lived. Not proud of that. But I felt sure she would have sent me special cards, cooked my favorite foods and generally made a fuss over me

Grandma didn't do any of those things. Instead, she smoked too much - Dad still loathed this with a passion and called her cigarettes 'cancer sticks', was, at least in in my estimation, an embarrassment in front of my friends and a bit of a nuisance. She liked to try on new tops that I'd bought with my hard-earned babysitting money and which were much too small for her, without asking; besides, she smelled of body odor. Or unplug my curling iron when I was scrambling around getting ready for a date and counting on a hot wand to work its magic and give me 'Farrah Fawcett hair' - then deny it! Always. I knew she was afraid of fires, especially a potential house fire. I did not know - or really care - why. If she was so afraid of something burning, I wondered, why did she often risk catastrophe by going to sleep with a cigarette in her mouth? Hypocrite. More than one set of my mother's good sheets were burned by this reckless practice.

To me, she was overweight, not especially clean and restless like an over-active child. She'd beg to come along to the movies with my sisters, then want to leave half-way through. Or we'd be out at a *very nice* restaurant for a Dinner and she'd get up - literally parting the table on one occasion, much to my mortification - to take *yet another* cigarette break.

We would see her two times a year, every year, for the Christmas and New Year's holidays at our house in northern California and always for a two-week stay with us in the summer at the cabin on Lake Vermilion. When she wasn't visiting, my folks would get a call from time to time about some disturbance she had caused, typically in the middle of the night, at one Midwestern hotel or another. She even re-married, but it was Britney-Spears-brief, (we never even knew his name), and was sporadically committed to various sanitariums. I recall one summer visiting her on the sprawling lawn of a rest home; I remember being anxious to leave. I have known the words *'manic depression'* for as long as I can remember and that, whatever that meant, it was what Grandma had -- and what made her act a little different. I was told more than once I should be *'understanding'.*

When I was in eighth grade my father went on sabbatical to England and so my mother, younger sister and I lived alongside him in a crowded flat at Churchill College, outside of damp and chilly Cambridge. On weekends we liked to take the train to London to sight-see, go to plays and out for Dinner. One Saturday afternoon a very handsome, debonair man joined us - apparently a second cousin of mine - Peter Kingman, my great Aunt Lucille's youngest son. (Lucille married a second time to a well-to-do older man she met while taking a mourning cruise to Hawaii. They made their family and life on the island of Oahu).

It was my first introduction to a *gentleman* and I have never, ever forgotten it. Having grown up in the mild California weather, I loathed the dreary London climate. I was pale from lack of sun, the roots of my fair hair turning a 'dirty dishwater' shade before my very eyes, which, once large and pleasing, now seemed to be sinking - and shrinking - into my forehead. My lips were too full, my teeth too large for my face.

My fashion sense was limited to my down ski jacket and a pair of 'Deckers'; multi-colored striped flip-flops that were popular when I was a young teen. Much to my children's horror, we actually called them 'thongs' back then. My father would admonish me every time I tried to leave our flat in them. Did he not understand that I really had nothing else to wear?

I was so terribly lonely; the proverbial ugly duckling before the swan. I remember aching with misery and longing, missing my friends and junior high school graduation, stuck at a new school with kids who made fun of my 'accent', and my lack of culture, which was evident on a daily basis. I'd get invited to a classmate's home for *tea*, for instance, and arrive fully-fed, thinking *tea* meant tea - and not Dinner.

I did not have anyone to talk to, anyone who *understood.* But Peter, in his cashmere overcoat and camel-colored ivy cap with a voice as smooth as Robert Wagner's, was the consummate escort and chaperone, thoroughly attentive and wonderful with this awkward pubescent version of me, linking his arm through mine and speaking to me very solicitously. I had never been treated like this before; I had never been around a true gentleman. By the end of the day I believed I might actually be special - *just maybe.* He asked me about the 'college' I attended in the English countryside, the uniform I had to wear - *boys!* - and what sort of music I liked. Then talk turned to his mother and my grandmother, our common bond.

"Did you know, Diane, that your grandmother was a very beautiful woman when she was young? As beautiful - or even more so - than almost any film star you can name? Have you seen the pictures of her? Why, she was legendary in her small town - and beyond.

...In fact, my mother, your Great Aunt Lucille, was admittedly quite jealous of your grandmother and her allure, as were the rest of the girls in their community. They wanted to look like Hadley Palmer. They wanted to *be* her".

He said this with awe; I heard it with skepticism. I was incredulous. I thought of the Grandma he was describing and, for the life of me, the two versions were entirely incongruent. Later Peter sent me a letter and a soft camel-colored ivy cap of my own, expensive, very similar to the one he had worn that day. I treasured this gift and gesture. When you are 'number three' out of four girls you get all too used to hand-me-downs and the assumption that you are nothing very special, interchangeable with the others and that by virtue of being in a long chain of same-sex siblings, you are at least a bit of a disappointment.

A few years later I had the pleasure of meeting Peter's two older brothers, Jim and John, who both made their homes on Oahu. I was there with a friend for my high school graduation trip and they, too, made me feel so special. John, who was number two out of three in their family, lamented about not feeling unique, either. We bonded over that. Bonded and boogie-boarded.

So I always remembered this exquisite gesture from a consummate gentleman and while I never saw Peter again, I never forgot how he treated me that day when I was at the height of my awkwardness -- or what he had to say about my grandmother.

Chapter Forty-Three

When I was sixteen my parents made the happy announcement we would be doing something new and different for the Christmas holiday: we would be spending it in Hawaii. *HAWAII!* I had never been there before and other than my interest in boys and cheerleading, being at the beach and soaking up the sun was absolutely at the top of my list of how I liked to spend my spare time. I wondered how Grandma would manage without us, but apparently I didn't need to worry: she would be coming along. *Oh, joy*! The one Christmas we *FINALLY* get to do something exciting and we are *STILL* tethered to Grandma, just like we were every summer in Minnesota. And, in fact, so would her older sister be joining us. I had never met my great aunt before and after the wonderful impression her youngest son had made on me, I was more than a little curious about her.

Lucille was pert and petite, carefully groomed - nothing like my grandmother - very tan with vivid green eyes and short, sprightly curls. She still lived on Oahu and flew to join the seven of us in Napili Bay off the coast of Maui. We had two adjoining condominiums. My parents, Aunt Lucille and Grandma stayed in one, while my three sisters and I shared the other. Lucille as it happened, had become hard of hearing - not unlike their late mother Bertha - and as the more mature of the two, still prone to believing she needed to manage our grandmother. I couldn't believe two old ladies would have so much to fight about, but they did. One exchange went like this:

Lucille to Grandma: "*Honey, you should have a sweater over your shoulders when we go to the restaurant... and leave the cigarettes behind, would you, Dear?*"

Grandma to Lucille: "*Oh, be quiet, Lucille! You are the bossiest thing!*" she grumbled.

Lucille back to Grandma: "*What was that you said, Honey? Can you repeat that; I couldn't hear you at all, Dear*".

And so on. You get the idea. Apparently the two of them - particularly Lucille, who only had sons and now, only grandsons - got a real kick out of *our* sisterly fights as well and mentioned this to my mother Shirley, who was probably laughing at the whole, ridiculous lot of us. Sisters...

When it was time to go on to Kauai, (Aunt Lucille pronounced it '*COW-eye'*), she flew back home to Oahu and we had our hands full now with Grandma. We were staying north but liked to drive the hour distance to Poipu Beach to snorkel and sunbathe in the afternoons. Grandma wasn't much for going in the water, yet she still needed something to do. So we bought her paperbacks - which she herself chose - and she read them quickly -- so voraciously, it seemed like she was going through about a book a day.

Flash-forward to a year later when I had to have my tonsils removed and required my own post-operative boredom reading material. Grandma's racy paperbacks were in our home and let me tell you, they were *really* steamy. They were bordering on erotic literature though frankly, there was nothing literary about them. My cheeks were swollen from my surgery and flaming crimson from the titillating content. (*WHY* would an old person like something like this? I wondered). It might have been then where I began to look at my grandma in a new way.

Chapter Forty-Four

And then I met Charlie. He was all dimples and edges, oozing sexuality and attitude. Confidentially, he was a bit of a bad boy or at the very least, a diamond-in-the-rough. In other words he was absolutely irresistible to a superficial teenage girl like myself and I was crazy about him. Enough to want to take him along on our annual summer vacation to the lake in Minnesota, which I had to convince my parents of. My dad, for one, saw right through this not yet cut diamond of mine: all the long six-hour drive from the Minneapolis airport, Dad lectured, then *QUIZZED,* my 'bad boy' about inorganic chemistry - ugh - when all Charlie wanted to do was make out with the professor's daughter.

Lake Vermilion has three hundred and sixty-five islands on it, though some are no bigger than a rock and a twig; an island for each day of the year. Charlie and I liked to take the speed boat off to one island or another for some privacy. My dad definitely kept a close eye on us and when Grandma arrived, she kept an eye on Charlie - specifically all the food he was consuming - while I kept my eye on my Grandma, and let me tell you, she knew her way around a man! Out came the sashay... the laughter... the *FLIRTING.*

She called him 'Chuck' right from the start and they really did like to banter back and forth. They could each give as good as they got:

"Chuck? I can call you Chuck, right, Chuck?" Grandma asked him saucily.

"I knew a guy who called me 'Chuck' once...

(long pause)

... He's dead now". Charlie deadpanned. A couple of seconds passed and Grandma laughed that beautiful lighthearted laughter of hers. He teased her mercilessly, especially if he was driving us somewhere and she sat shotgun; he liked to pretend we were lost, just to get a rise of panic from her. And he was an impeccable mimic. Grandma giggled at his antics and impressions like a smitten school girl.

"Why Shirley, that boy is going to eat you out of house and home. He has already had six pieces of fruit today and it's only early afternoon", she'd say to my mother much too loudly. (Did she not think we could hear her?) Mom, accustomed to four perpetually dieting, weight-conscious daughters, was thrilled to have someone who actually ate, and tried her best to shush her. Our cabin was small, with no dishwasher and when it was my turn to clean up the kitchen, Grandma would study my sillouette and say to my mom - again, believing I couldn't hear, I suppose -

'Diane is so pretty. Just look at her tiny waist. She could be Miss America'.

And finally to me,

"*You are so pretty. You could be Miss America*".

Her compliments warmed my heart and gave me a welcome boost of confidence: finally, Grandma had taken an interest in me... or maybe it was my boyfriend Charlie - Chuck - who had captured her attention. They took walks, picked berries and went for paddleboat rides, even played poker together. Charlie was older than I, already over twenty-one, and he and Grandma liked to have a bottle of beer - or two or three - down by the dock before the sunset. Drinking buddies.

"You like cars, Chuck". It was more a statement than a question. And speaking of cars, I don't recall a single time that summer where my grandma climbed inside the passenger seat and pouted. Besides, 'Chuck' would never have let her.

"He reminds me of someone..."

Chapter Forty-Five

The summer I was twenty Grandma had another bad car accident. She was driving her latest Ford Pinto down to Liberty for a visit with my Mom's younger sister Jeanie when she saw a large box in the middle of the road, swerved to avoid hitting it and ran into a guard rail instead. She was banged up pretty badly, requiring another stay in the county hospital, Lincoln General.

My parents were in Europe at the time, my older sisters working. Mom called long-distance from Paris, asking if she gave me her credit card number and arranged some traveler's checks at our bank, would I please fly to Nebraska and stay with Grandma for the next two weeks?

Young and in love, it was about the last thing in the world I felt like doing and besides, it would cut short my vacation from college, (which I did not like and was dreading going back to). But how do you say 'no' to your mother? Mine is an angel who will do anything for anyone and I could not. Next thing I knew I was on a plane, bound for Lincoln, headed toward extreme heat, oppressive humidity, flying away from my boyfriend and entering into the company of someone I still had little use for and even less in common with. Or so I thought.

When I arrived at the hospital and entered Grandma's private room, I should have been overwhelmed by the atmosphere. Bright lights, an odious antiseptic smell and intimidating monitors are frightening to most, yet I was oddly comforted by this environment. I felt pretty badly though for Grandma: she had IVs in both arms, her head wrapped in gauze, oxygen tubes up her nostrils, a black eye and a bruised cheek. She looked so much smaller and more vulnerable than I could ever remember. Apparently she lost quite a lot of weight prior to the accident. I suspected that her previous summer with 'Chuck' may have spurred her to take a renewed interest in herself.

Her eyes fluttered when she heard my voice. She seemed surprised to see me. I bent down and carefully kissed her good cheek, then told her I would be there during the daytime to keep her company and in the evenings I would stay at her house in Beatrice, bring in her mail, straighten up and water the lawn. This seemed to please her and she wondered aloud when she might be well enough to play 'Hearts', a card game she had taught me when I was a little girl, 'or maybe 'War'. For some reason we both chuckled; for some reason, as restless as Grandma always acted, she had nonetheless always had the patience for a long and hearty round of War.

The nurse came in and shooed me away so she could give Grandma her daily sponge bath. I wandered the halls beyond her hospital wing and when I thought I had killed enough time for the nurse to have helped Grandma complete her grooming, I started back for her room. I was distracted. The movie Terms of Endearment, with Shirley McClaine, Debra Winger *and* Jack Nicholson had been filmed in this very hospital a year earlier. The place was still teeming with excitement.

I had been admiring a landscape on one of the walls so admittedly, I wasn't looking where I was going as I should have been. I was fairly startled to bump right into an older gentleman carrying flowers, evidently coming from the opposite direction. He was wearing a smart trilby hat and looked like Cary Grant appeared in his old age, tall, with vivid brows, pleasing brown eyes and a shock of white hair. He had a deep voice and smelled of Old Spice. He must have been *very handsome* back in his day, I thought to myself.

"Oh my goodness, I'm so sorry", I exclaimed, remembering my manners a bit too late. He was already bent down, trying to retrieve his bouquet. "Oh gosh, I have totally ruined your flowers!" I apologized. He was trying to straighten the arrangement, flustered himself, but also quick to reassure me.

"Don't worry, young lady; don't you give it a second thought. It was just an accident... But I'm afraid I may have to buy some more flowers".

“Can I help you? Can I at least contribute to the cost?” I offered, bending down alongside him, reaching inside my purse for my billfold.

“Please, young lady, don’t give it another thought though, if you know how to find it, do you think you could lead me to the hospital gift shop?” he inquired.

“You know, I’m not that familiar with this place and I should really be getting back to my grandmother...”

“Well, never mind then, I’m sure I can find it. Besides, I doubt they have violets, and that’s the flower I’ll be wanting”.

“Oh, that’s really too bad. I feel awful about this.

I hope you find what you’re looking for...”

“Me too”, he agreed congenially, tipping his hat. He may have winked.

And then he was gone.

Chapter Forty-Six

Grandma seemed to be getting a little bit better every day. She was down to a single IV, acting more alert, her black eye becoming a soft purple. The shade reminded me of a pretty wildflower and recalled my chance meeting with the mysterious older gentleman. Grandma was talkative now, eager for some company. (Privately, I have always struggled with shyness. When I got older, I would think nothing of leading fifty or more people at a time through a yoga class, but put me one-on-one in a cocktail party setting, and I am painfully uncomfortable, *awkward* even). After the preliminaries I couldn't really think of what to say - afraid I was in for a long, tedious afternoon of boring chatter - so I decided to tell her about bumping into this man and how he'd been looking for violets, which was unusual to me as they are wild flowers and wilt too easily -- certainly less-than-ideal to be part of any floral arrangement. Grandma looked far away for a moment.

"I used to like violets".

"Who knows, Grandma? Maybe it's time for a boyfriend!" I joked. She laughed at this - I did love the sound of her musical laughter - and asked me how things were going with my 'Chuck'. I confided to her that I was definitely in love with him - how he may just be 'the one' - but as I was still so young, I was afraid perhaps the feelings we had for each other wouldn't last.

"What do you mean? You think you might grow tired of each other?" she wondered.

I nodded feebly and told her then of a striking young couple I had seen at the beach a few years earlier when I was sunbathing with my girlfriends. What an impression they made on me! I just couldn't take my eyes off them, openly staring and watching – fascinated - as they interacted with one another throughout the day. The man was tall and blonde, with a Tom Selleck mustache; the woman tiny, with long dark hair and exotic blue eyes. They had a little girl - fair, like the man - and the striking woman spent much of the day playing with the child, making sand castles and looking for sea shells by the water. She was so *attentive.* She held the little girl's hand and kept looking back, blowing kisses to her lover.

It all looked so terribly romantic - *so devoted* - nothing like any relationship I'd ever had or seen before, certainly one that included children, and I announced to my friends that I wanted *exactly* that kind of special closeness with the guy I ultimately fell for 'someday'. "Yeah, well, Good Luck with that!" my girlfriends teased me. They clearly felt like that kind of thing was unattainable as well, as unattainable as the woman's stunning body.

A year later my friends and I were back at the beach and saw that same family. The little girl was taller now, missing her two front teeth; the gorgeous woman more impossibly tiny now and more stunning, this time attired in an eye-catching canary yellow bikini, with long strings that were tied at her waist. But despite her head-turning beauty, this time the man ignored her - and she him - throughout the afternoon. Gone were the air-blown kisses, affection and constant checking on each other. They seemed both bored and irritated and the woman did not dote on the little girl nearly as much as she had the previous Spring. I was up at the restroom later that day waiting in a long line when I noticed this woman waiting in line with her daughter a few people ahead of me; I was close enough that I overheard her speaking to her companion.

I could tell by what she said to her friend that, apparently, she and the handsome man were not married after all; she was not even this little girl's mother! Turns out, they had been dating for a just over a year and the relationship had become strained -- as had clearly been evident to me from watching their body language. So my illusions of perfect, romantic love were shattered that day, almost as quickly as they had been inspired.

"Now I don't know *what* to believe about love", I concluded.

Grandma studied me for a long moment. It felt like she was looking at me, *SEEING* me, for the very first time.

"So you are a romantic", she declared and she became thoughtful. Finally she took a breath and said,

"I think I know exactly what you mean. I used to have grand illusions of a grand love, but they only brought me grand heartbreak in the end".

"With Grandpa Perry?" I asked, a bit mortified.

"No, Doll, it was someone before his time... then for one brief, shining moment, afterwards too".

The admission hung there in the air, but Grandma said nothing more. I had been taught by my mother to never ask a forward question, so we were both silent. I thought she must be getting tired and it might be time for the nurse to check her vitals and give Grandma her pain medication. Finally,

"He used to bring me violets..."

Now it was my turn to appraise her, and I realized in that moment that however well I thought I'd known my grandma all these years, I really didn't know her at all. Peel away the extra pounds, the grey hair and years of life - and heartache - and suddenly we had a lot more in common than I thought. We were merely, simply two females reassessing one another. But before I could say anything more the nurse came in, so I excused myself and went in search of the hospital cafeteria. By the time I got back, Grandma's day nurse, Bobbie Ray, met me at the door.

"Mrs. Wallace is resting comfortably now. Let's let her sleep, shall we?"

It was the first time in my entire life when a conversation with my grandma that had been cut short felt like a disappointment to me. I drove my Aunt Jeanie's car back to Grandma's house and felt lonely for her company the rest of that long, hot afternoon. I meandered from room to room, picking up framed photographs of my dad and his sister, laying down on Aunt Dolly's bed, listless, the smooth satin spread cool beneath my skin, not knowing quite what to do with myself. It felt long and lonely to me because all the sudden, I really liked my grandma - and missed her company terribly.

Chapter Forty-Seven

Trading stories. This was how we related to one another now. I would share something Charlie had done and Grandma would tell me a tidbit or two about her first beau. Turns out, they had something in common: both had a thing for cars. Grandma wondered aloud what kinds of mischievous activities we liked to do. ("Cow-tipping?" she suggested). She was nostalgic, evidently a much more natural conversationalist than I, and I appreciated the playfulness of her question - she did know how to break the ice - and could not resist sharing one of our more recent escapades. I had convinced Charlie we should tee-pee (*'you know what it means to tee-pee someone's house, Grandma*?' to which she merely nodded; I must say, I was impressed), the house of a former boyfriend of mine who had not been particularly nice about our break up: he kept calling my home then hanging up on me, and I had caught him - more than once - spying outside my upstairs bedroom window. Kind of creepy. I thought it was time for a dose of his own medicine; he was asking for it. Charlie agreed and was game for this, so he rounded up some friends of his to help us with our mission. One summer evening we drove to this ex-boyfriend's house in the middle of the night in his friend's old brown van wearing dark clothing, armed with several rolls of toilet paper and some shaving cream.

'We climbed out of the vehicle as quietly as we could and scattered ourselves throughout the property so that we might make a sound effort and thoroughly cover the house, trees and backyard with toilet paper. Most of us had sweatshirts on - 'hoodies' - to better camouflage ourselves.

We were having a great time - naturally a little afraid, but of course that only heightened our sense of pleasure - and when we were satisfied with our job, we all climbed back into the van and sped off. Darren was driving, Charlie rode shotgun with the rest of us in the two rows of seats behind them. At some point Charlie turned around to take a head count - he wanted to be sure no one had been left behind - yet he realized, astonished, that we had more passengers than we'd started with! What the heck? All of a sudden, one of our 'friends' pulled off his hoodie and yelled,

"BUSTED!"

It was actually my ex-boyfriend's father, and let me tell, you, Grandma, my stomach went to my throat from the shock! He wasn't really mad, but after he revealed himself, he did make us drive him back to his house to clean up our masterpiece. Apparently he had heard us and thought it would be great payback to come out to join us, 'aiding and abetting' us in our crime of passion" I told her.

"Outrageous!" my grandma exclaimed. She actually tried to slap her knee, but her remaining IV prevented this, and she giggled and giggled in that wonderful, musical way of hers. There was glee - and approval - in her lovely grey eyes. She was shaking with mirth and wiping tears from her eyes; she'd laughed *that* hard.

"Oh, we loved that kind of mischief as well back in my day! My old flame used to call me his 'partner in crime' she beamed. When Grandma told me about Ari, I could tell from the look on her face, the way her eys lit up and her voice changed, that he was really something special and I said felt so badly they didn't get to end up together -- that they never got their happy ending.

"...But then YOU wouldn't be here, not to mention your father or your sisters", Grandma reminded me, patting my knee.

"...And Aunt Dolly" I pointed out. Grandma winced, but I don't think it was from the pain.

Bobbie Ray was in the room along with us now, straightening up and listening in; she had a story of her own to share. She told us how her daughter Monique had recently had 'the most precious baby girl' and that mother and baby already demonstrated they shared a unique bond: when Monique was pregnant with her little girl, according to her husband Steve, she used to stick an arm straight up in the air and curl the fingers of her hand into a fist, then fall asleep that way. It seemed strange to him -- and not entirely comfortable. He had never seen his wife do this before her pregnancy, or after.

"...Wouldn't you know", Bobbie Ray laughed, "Her baby Tanya was just a few days old when, lo and behold, she stuck her tiny arm straight up in the air, curled the fist of that hand and went to sleep, same way as her Mama. Now THAT'S a bond!" she chuckled.

After Bobbie Ray had left the room Grandma looked at me, hard, and for a moment she looked just like my father. She said she had never felt that way about her own - and only - daughter. It hurt me for Dolly to hear her mother - my grandma - admit this out loud; it was one thing to sense this painful elephant in the room, but now Grandma had admitted as much.

My own mother was wonderful to each of her four daughters, and thus it was difficult for me to understand how Grandma could be this way. I felt familiar with her now, not nearly as bashful, and so I rather bluntly asked her how she could be so fine with us, her granddaughters, and not feel this way about her own daughter.

"But you have always been *so good* to us!" I reminded her.

"Yes, but it was different with you girls: you were PJ and Shirley's daughters, and I knew your parents would do right by you; I just got to spoil you four. But Dolly was my own, with no one else, save Perry, to take an interest in her... and the last time I had felt such a protectiveness toward a female creature - my favored baby sister Buddy - it had all gone so horribly wrong... I couldn't trust myself with that feminine responsibility ever, ever again".

It was as big and as honest an admission as I ever thought I'd hear and I felt an overwhelming sense of compassion for my grandmother, for Dolly and for poor Buddy, whose name I had never heard Grandma say aloud before. I needed to sit with this for a while. Suddenly things were feeling heavy.

Chapter Forty-Eight

By Friday of the second week, Grandma was well enough to be discharged from Lincoln General and I pushed her wheelchair to the curb, where my aunt's car was waiting. It was time to go home for *both* of us. When I got back to our house in California, Mom told me how proud she was of me and how well I had handled the whole situation. Grandma stayed in Beatrice, healing, but not too long after she was out of the woods, she came down with a mysterious sore throat, one that just wouldn't go away on its own. After nine months of this and suffering mostly in silence, Grandma finally told her doctor, who decided she should have her tonsils out.

I was back at college, in my dorm, when Mom called me with the news.

"Do you want me to go out and stay with her again?" I offered.

Mom seemed surprised. She remembered all the times I'd complained about Grandma; this turn of emotion was something new for me.

"No, Honey. You need to stay in school. Kate wants to go".

"Oh", was all I replied. I felt suddenly, overwhelmingly jealous of my older sister, that she was finished with college, which I really disliked, and this was another thing I found out Grandma and I shared in common. I had confided to her the previous summer that I just didn't see the point of it - and particularly my English major - telling her how much I despised Shakespeare.

She told me then that when Grandpa Perry came to Chicago and proposed to her she was in the midst of her first mid-terms, and the temptation of leaving all the studying and pressure was just too great, so she accepted. I really thought that was all there was to the story; it would have been enough for me, and envious that Kate and Grandma had always had something special.

The tonsillectomy wasn't enough to solve Grandma's health woes, however. Her doctor discovered she had lymphoma; apparently her 'cancer sticks' were aptly named and had, indeed, caught up with her. We were all saddened and concerned by this latest development. The following summer she was being treated with radiation and chemotherapy. This time I insisted I fly out to Beatrice.

"Grandma would want me to!" I declared to my mother.

"But Honey, it really isn't necessary: Grandma has round-the-clock nurses at her house ("*Spending Perry's money faster than he could* ever *make it, per usual*", piped in my dad), including Bobbie Ray, and while I'm sure she would appreciate your offer, she knows you have a full-time job at the preschool. She doesn't want you to drop everything for her".

"Well, can I go for my vacation then? I can pay for my ticket with some of my paychecks". I was plaintive.

"Why, Ditty-Diane" (Mom's pet name for me), "What has gotten into you?" Mom knew how much I valued my income, that I couldn't wait to spend any money I had made at the local mall.

"You sound like a changed person when it comes to your grandmother".

"Is there something wrong with that?" I asked a bit sharply. "You've always lectured me about my attitude with Grandma. You should be happy I've had a change of heart!"

"I am, Honey. And if it would really mean this much to you to visit then, yes, I think you should go out to see her". It was settled then.

When I arrived at her house in Beatrice I gave my grandma a tender kiss and gently touched her head, with its thinning hair, the way she had loved me to do for her when I was a girl. Her skull felt as fragile as one my little preschooler's, and my heart swelled with protectiveness. Still, I could see my mom was right: Grandma's rotation of nurses had everything well in hand after all. There wasn't much for me to do other than keep Grandma company. We played Hearts and War; Grandma asked me to go out and get her some Kentucky Fried Chicken, which was still her favorite. Because the nurses were there 24-7, we were never really alone and as such our conversations remained surface, lacking the depth and substance of the previous summer.

Aunt Dolly, who was divorced and lived in southern California - had for many years now - never came to see her but she did send long, hand-written letters to the house nearly every day. Grandma would instruct the nurse on duty to throw each one in the trash, unopened, ("*Well, you know where that goes*" she'd say with a chuckle).

This family legacy of mothers and daughters not understanding each other would never be healed, so it seemed, and neither would my Grandmother's lymphoma. Bobbie Ray felt a bit uncomfortable tossing aside unopened letters - you could tell from the way she spoke about them all how close she was to her own family - and she chuckled weakly now to break the tension, I suppose.

"And she never accepts her gentleman caller's visits, either", Bobbie Ray chided.

I looked up from the Ladies' Home Journal I'd been reading.

"Grandma has a gentleman caller?" I asked, a little more than somewhat surprised. "Who is he,

Bobbie Ray?" Grandma's pet nurse didn't answer.

"He brings your grandmother violets, but she won't allow us to let him in the house". Bobbie Ray interjected. "Isn't that strange? Not his bringing flowers to a lady, mind you -- and such a fine and upstanding one as your grandmother. But why violets? They're nothing more than glorified weeds!"

"Not so", Grandma disagreed, shaking her head. "I think they're beautiful. Always have".

"Grandma, who is he?" I repeated.

She said nothing. But she stared at me for a long time. Finally she confided in a quiet voice,

"I don't look the way I used to".

In spite of the artificial breeze and offensive rattling noise coming from her home air-conditioner, the admission still hung there in the thick Nebraska air, gathering heat inside my ears - until it was deafening. To Grandma's credit, that's as close as she ever came to telling me she had once been a beautiful woman. Modesty truly is a virtue and it certainly was one of hers.

I thought if I could just get some time alone with her, I could convince my grandma to love her daughter better and that, just maybe, she would finish the story about Ari and their broken romance. Finally, I got my opportunity.

Chapter Forty-Nine

I think Bobbie Ray sensed that I wanted some time alone with my grandma before I had to go back home to California. So she made up some excuse about needing Tuesday morning off to take her husband to the dentist. Would I mind very much driving Grandma to her chemotherapy, Bobbie Ray wondered.

I jumped at the opportunity; aware that my vacation days were nearly over, I figured this might be my only chance to talk to Grandma - *really* talk to her - one-on-one. I had so many questions! I couldn't stop thinking about Ari and why they hadn't stayed together -- especially now when it was evident to me that he was Grandma's gentleman caller, and surely the man I'd bumped into at the hospital the year prior. Why was my grandmother being so stubborn about him?

I drove Grandma in her wintergreen Pinto, with its conspicuous white racing stripes, to chemotherapy and accompanied her inside the treatment center. There were patients in various stages of sickness and shades of palor: some with light blue masks covering their mouths and noses, some without hair, or wearing scarves or wigs or hats; most of them had a companion of some kind to sit with them and help keep them comfortable. We got there a little early and had to wait for a bit until Grandma's nurse was ready for her. When it was her turn to be hooked up, Grandma opted for a chair near the window, instead of a private room with a bed and consequently we were facing an elderly man, who was also a patient, and his wide-eyed wife.

I found myself watching them interact, in much the same way as I had watched that beautiful sun-kissed couple at the beach a few years earlier. And I was in awe of them, especially the man and the care with which he treated his dainty wife. He was making *such* a fuss over her - he was, after all, the patient - and insisted the nurse bring her some Oreos and a box of juice. *Pre-school fare.*

Even as they hooked him up to receive his 'poison', the gentleman kept asking after his sweetheart, adamant that she have her morning snack; you'd have thought those Oreos were the most important thing in the world by his reaction! I do believe it was the most romantic thing I have ever witnessed, and I found myself spellbound. Grandma wasn't getting any attention from me but when I finally turned to her, I noticed she was watching them as well. Tender. That's what they were. I wondered to myself if the woman was worthy of all this; it seemed so one-sided. And again, HE was the one who was sick.

"She's awfully lucky, isn't she?" Grandma asked me rhetorically, not waiting for an answer. Not needing one, as if she'd read my mind.

"He must be a reverend, or something like that, don't you think?" I asked her.

Grandma's nurse overheard my question and said no, he wasn't. He was just an ordinary man and an extraordinary husband who knew he was very sick and did not have too much longer. It was his mission to protect his wife with every ounce of strength he had left.

"Wow" I said, chastened. "What must it feel like to be loved like that? To be so cherished" I wondered. Grandma got that far way look in her eyes. After a bit she said, very quietly,

"I remember being cherished that way. Someday, Doll, I'll tell you about it - *maybe*".

"Grandma, I'd love nothing more than to hear all about him, but I'm going home soon; it's now or never". I reminded her.

"Oh", was all she said in response.

But suddenly my grandma was far, far away.

When she and I got back to her house it was starting to rain, a gentle summertime storm, and we took refuge. Grandma was tired and a bit nauseous. I offered to make her tea and some dry toast and tried to help her into bed. She liked to watch a game show - *any* game show -

from the old black-and-white television her bedroom.

She soon fell asleep; I could hear her snoring softly from the front parlor. I went to check on her and tucked a light quilt around her midsection. She looked so soft, so fragile -- she didn't have a single line or wrinkle, even though she was more than seventy years old. Bobbie Ray checked in by phone mid-afternoon. Apparently her husband had had a bad reaction at the dentist and she really did need to stay with him, if that was alright. I said yes, of course we'd be fine here; Grandma and me.

I went onto Grandma's front porch and took a deep breath, inhaling the fresh post-rain air. It smelled incredible, but the sky was still dark -- and I thought we might be in for something more serious. So I went back inside, got her car keys and drove to the local market to collect a few things. I pulled into Kentucky Fried Chicken for a bucket of chicken, in case she was hungry for something more than toast when she woke up. Grandma still adored fried chicken with biscuits and gravy.

When I got back to the house, she was stirring. I wondered aloud if she would like me to draw her a hot bath. Grandma said, 'mmm, that sounded good', so I went upstairs and opened her bathroom cabinets searching for her Vita-Bath, a foamy green gel that she always asked for for Mother's Day.

Imagine my surprise when the cabinet beheld fifty or more bottles: that stuff was expensive, difficult for my mother to find, and here Grandma had *years'* worth. Clearly she didn't need any more Vita-Bath -- though she asked for it every Mother's Day and Birthday; clearly the supply she had on hand would outlast my grandma. I felt sad... and dismayed. Would I ever *really* understand my grandmother?

When the tub was full, I went to get Grandma and helped her undress and into the water. I was uncomfortable seeing her naked - I myself have always been very modest - so looked away as best I could, focusing on my bare legs. I was wearing white cotton shorts and was a bit distressed that my hard-earned tan might have faded -- combining a moment of vanity with an awkward attempt to preserve her dignity, all the while still trying to supervise her.

It occurred to me that it might be nice to light a few candles. I even found a small portable radio and turned it on to an 'oldies' station. Grandma eased her way in and finally rested her head against the lip of the claw foot bath tub. She closed her eyes and after a bit her face softened to repose. She looked like she might have gone to sleep again.

"Can I get you anything else, Grandma?" I asked her. "Maybe some iced tea?" I suggested.

"No, Doll, Thank-you anyway; this is more than enough for now. You spoil me". Grandma smiled. Her eyes were still closed however.

I was sitting on the closed seat of the toilet, looking down at my hands now and wondering what to do with myself. Wondering, fleetingly, what Charlie was doing right at that moment back in California. I half-stood so I could raise the pink and white chenille curtain with its soft pompons, which seemed like cotton balls, a smidge to take a peak at the weather. It still looked threatening. I had almost given up on any meaningful conversation and was keenly aware that this was my second-to-last evening there. Grandma took me by surprise then:

"Ari used to spoil me so..." she confided. "He used to do the most wonderful, thoughtful, *playful* things for me...

...just like that gentleman at the treatment center who made such a fuss over his wife this morning. Ari was like that, only sexier".

I had to laugh: tender and dear as the 'reverend' was to his bride, he was anything but sexy. After a bit I said shyly,

"Do you want to tell me about Ari now?"

"... Grandma?" I asked, sitting back down on the toilet.

She seemed to be ignoring my questions.

"Brush my hair for me, Doll. Rub my neck and shoulders". Even if she said nothing more, it was my pleasure to do this for her and when I saw the expression of rapture on her face, I thought, I could do this one thing for my grandmother for hours -- for the rest of her life, if that was what she wanted.

"Did Ari used to rub your neck?" I asked her finally. Timidly.

Grandma nodded. "He did", she agreed. "He cherished me; he *adored* me..."

"Tell me, Grandma," I implored. "Tell me all about Ari, about what you loved so much about him -- and why, if you did, why you left him".

She opened her eyes for a moment.

"Is tonight your last night here?" she asked me.

I shook my head.

"No. Tomorrow night is". I answered.

"Well, then" she responded.

And then she *did*. Grandma sat in that tub with her eyes closed and the three candles flickering, and she told me about her first love... about Ari's mother... about her mama... and finally, about Buddy. Grandma - for whatever reason - spared me no detail, and I was hungry for every single morsel she could provide, trying to listen -- as well as sear it all into my memory.

She told me about the Hough barn and their bold, clandestine romance - *the lovemaking* - and I was completely spellbound by her descriptions. I was twenty-one years *young* at the time but already aware that I was too old - and too demure - to ever have an encounter such as hers, one so illicit, yet even more, so passionate and all-encompassing. When Grandma got to the part about Buddy, I was grateful that she still had her eyes closed; I was brushing tears away from my own, almost overcome now by my own emotion.

Grandma stopped talking. She opened her eyes, propping herself up with the agility of a much younger, lighter - unencumbered - woman. When she did this, the water sloshed loudly, which startled me. Then she turned around to look at me very studiously and at last she said:

"I have never, *ever,* told anyone about that before. Naturally, I could not tell Perry. Never my folks -- though I am certain my mother knew about it in her own way... not even Lucille. At times I thought I was going mad from the secrecy and the shame. What a great relief it is to finally tell someone!" she stated. "*You*".

I was still swatting tears away, blinking rapidly, trying to regain my composure. I looked back at her just as emphatically and said,

"Thank-you, Grandma Hadley. Thank-you from the bottom of my heart. I feel grateful you chose *ME* to share it with, and I will never, *ever* forget it".

"Alright, Doll. Let's get an old, ridiculous tub-o-lard out of this tub; I'm afraid I am starting to prune".

And that was all.

...Or so I thought.

Chapter Fifty

Grandma died in late-May of 1988. Those cancer sticks got her in the end, after all. She was seventy-four years old at the time of her death; I was twenty-three. My dad, in his *particular way*, said something I felt was unkind and thus deterred me from flying out to Nebraska for Grandma's funeral. By the time he called to apologize, it was too late. The damage had been done and I wouldn't change my mind. Besides, I consoled myself, I'd already said and heard everything I needed as it pertained to my grandma from my grandmother herself.

My parents and two older sisters went out to Nebraska for the Memorial Day Weekend. Dolly refused to attend. I thought about my grandma over that holiday and prayed she was in a better place, off her proverbial rocking chair of shame and deeply buried grief, the one that had shackled her in penitence and kept her from living a full, happy life. And even more, from really being able to love. I thought of something Grandma told me later, sometime after her bathtub confession, when she'd said:

"Grief waits for you"

I did not fully understand this statement at the time, took it to mean a pejorative 'you', as I was still too young and unaffected by life's inevitable rhythms and challenges. By my late-forties, however, my own heart had been strained more than a few times. Her observation resonated with me much more personally. Deeply.

I had been married to Charlie for more than two decades and we had two nearly-grown children when I finally made my way back to Nebraska, back to tiny Liberty - by myself - for a family reunion on my mother's side. My husband was busy starting a new company, our son had his first fulltime job as a lifeguard and our daughter was off at theatre camp, so I rented a car for that weekend, unsure of how I'd feel being around cousins and relatives I hadn't seen in years and needing to maintain some sort of independence, uncomfortable in the summer heat - *still* no good at small talk.

The reunion was boring for me. I didn't recognize or even know most of the attendants. I was missing my family and our life at home, missing my yoga students and big classes. I didn't think anyone there would notice my absence so I quietly made my way out of the venue and drove down the dusty highway heading toward the old Liberty cemetery. I actually *liked* cemeteries -- maybe even more than I liked hospitals. While my son was a toddler and afraid of the slides and swings at our local park, I used to take him to this old historical cemetery near our home, and he and I would walk around the grounds while he pushed his little red wheelbarrow. Odd, I can see that now. We probably looked like a grieving young widow and son.

The day was hot, hot, HOT: when I stepped out of my rental car, it felt like I was setting foot into my hot yoga studio back in California. I was already beginning to sweat profusely, risking ruination of the delicate fabric of my new sundress. My make-up was melting, my mood wilting. I wondered how long I could last outside. There was a strong, dry wind blowing all around me. I still liked to wear my hair quite long - Grandma would probably have had something to say about that - and the wind was causing it to swirl around in the air, which somehow only made me feel hotter and more irritated.

I knew I wouldn't find my grandma there. She had been buried in Omaha more than twenty years earlier alongside Grandpa Perry - rightly so - but I thought I might just find Buddy's grave if I could withstand the blazing temperature. The tale about the school children and their torment of my father, my aunt and most of all, my late, great aunt still haunted me. Perhaps I should have stopped in the woods for some violets I could bring to her. I knew Grandma would appreciate this gesture.

So that's what I did. In spite of the heat and my discomfort, I took time to find a handful of purple flowers from a nearby field and carried them to my late aunt's grave, which I found after a little searching. Intense emotion stirred inside me as I placed them at her lonesome plot which was abandoned, save for some sprigs of moss bursting optimistically through cracks in the tired gray stone. The wind was blowing more aggressively now and I tried to make a makeshift ponytail, securing my wayward hair with my other hand as I kneeled down to look at her picture.

I studied her portrait, scratched and weather-worn, the enamel close to decay. I offered up my other hand with its fistful of purple weeds and tried to visit with her. At first I really didn't know *what* to say, other than to tell her how pleased I was to finally be making her acquaintance, something I'd been saying all afternoon at the reunion. I told her that I wished I could have known her, how I loved to draw - as she had - and that I was so sorry about the tragic fire which had claimed her young life.

A warm, gentle breeze swirled around me then. I felt an undeniable presence and a sense of peace... as well as loss. I can't say it was loneliness for my grandma I was feeling - she'd been gone so many years by now - but I felt lonely nonetheless. I have never cried easily, yet I was crying now.

At first it was just a few tears but then I cried harder, provoked by both the heat and the stark tragedy of it all. *The regret.* I was hot and sweaty, raw with emotion and the weight of Grandma's remorse, nearly overcome, as if the story were of *my* life, not hers. I was so exposed that it embarrassed me, terribly, when another car pulled up and a stout old woman with thick, fleshy legs and elbows climbed out. I am sure I looked a fright and this was an inopportune time, to say the least, to find myself in the presence of a stranger. I reached for my oversize designer sunglasses hoping, at the very least, to conceal my red eyes, my no-doubt smeared mascara and streaked cheeks.

Nebraskans are nothing if not friendly and hospitable. Of course this lady was no different. She was talking to me now, having a full-blown conversation that evidently I was a part of and I got up from Buddy's grave hastily, brushing my knees with my hands and wiping the evidence of sorrow from the rest of my face as discreetly as I could. I started nodding in ascension - which had seemed to work for me at the reunion - but then I realized she was actually asking me questions: 'Who was I? How did I know about Buddy?' She sounded both bossy and out of breath.

So I explained that I was in town for the Thomas family reunion, invited by my aunt Jeanie, but I was also related, on my other side, my father's side, to the late Florence Jean Palmer. She was my would-have-been great aunt -- and that my great, great uncle Roy had written a letter to my parents, (I still have saved it in my baby book), that I was the spitting image of her, except for my blonde hair. I told her I was Hadley Palmer Wallace's granddaughter -- and I said it without shame or hesitation.

"Ari's girl?" she interrupted.

"You know about Ari?" I asked, doubtful. "About Ari... and Hadley?"

"Of course I do!" she laughed. "Well, maybe not *personally*, but they were legendary. Everyone who grew up in these parts knew about Ari and Hadley, about what a golden couple they were once-upon-a-time-ago.

I am Virgil Hough's oldest daughter Margo, and Ari was my second cousin. He's buried here, don'tcha know?" she asked in that small town twang.

Stupefied, I merely shook my head.

"I--I didn't realize he was... dead" I answered limply. (But of course he would be, I reminded myself too late: by now, if he were still alive, Arlington Hough would be over one hundred years old).

"Oh, cousin Ari died so many years ago. Lung cancer. He was a chronic cigarette smoker most of his life" she chuckled regretfully, "but I think he really died of a broken heart".

“Really? Do you *really* think so?” I asked, skeptic. “I heard he married and lived in Europe, that he was very successful”.

“But he never got over his first love, don’tcha know?”

I said nothing; what was there to say?

“Does anyone?” she asked, though more to herself it seemed. “Would you like me to show you cousin Ari’s grave? It’s quite impressive”.

She was a little pushy, but I was beyond intrigued and so I nodded as she pulled my arm and led me, trance-like, in another direction.

Naturally Ari’s plot was large and expansive, like everything else my grandmother had told me about him and his prominent family. It stated his full name, Arlington Rufus Hough, the dates of his birth and his death, and the various roles he had served throughout his lifetime: son; husband; father; grandfather; friend. It did not state his occupation or that Ari had been a very successful businessman. It didn’t need to. The massive plot and accompanying border said this better than any inscription might have done.

I felt less diffident now, perhaps emboldened by… I don’t know what, exactly. Just emboldened. Something new for me.

“I know he didn’t like his first name”. Margo told me.

“What makes you say that?” I asked her.

"Well, it was a well-known fact when he was a youth that he was teased for it; too much of a mouthful. Too fancy. Besides, look at the inscription at the bottom corner of his tomb: '*Eternally Harry'*. I mean, a guy's gotta really hate his name to want to change it so... permanently".

I kneeled so that I might run my hand along the personal inscription, which had been etched in different script. I traced the letters with my index finger, allowing it to linger there. Finally, I turned my head back to Margo who was still standing. I noticed then how very large her knees were - they matched her elbows - and hoped she hadn't seen me staring at them.

"Well, how do you know it was *his* idea?" I asked, breaking my own thoughts. "I mean, he is dead after all -- so I would assume anything put on his headstone was someone else's idea... like perhaps his wife's". I was feeling really bold now.

"For starters", Margo explained, getting her dander up just a bit, "Ari was divorced a long, long time ago. And I can see why you would draw that conclusion - about most people - but Ari wasn't like most people. Add to that, he knew he was going to die. He was sick with lung cancer for over two years and had plenty of time to get his affairs in order. And he was sick of being under his mother's thumb his entire life; there was no way he was going to take *that* into eternity". She softened then, shaking her head and chuckling ironically.

"Is that its only significance?" I challenged. It wasn't like me to be this forward, to be playing Devil's advocate, especially with someone I'd only just met. But I just felt like there was *something more* to it. Call it my female intuition. And I was living in the pop culture era of international super stars Brad Pitt and Angelina Jolie, whose coupledom had been famously coined 'Brangelina' some time ago, so naturally I was hopeful that 'Harry' might likewise for him and my grandmother. For Ari and Hadley.

"Well of course! Whatever else could it be?" Margo retorted, as if I'd just asked her the world's most absurd question. She was losing interest in me and likely irritable from this terrible heat, as was I - it was still 'hotter than Hades' as my mother would say - so Margo bade me goodbye and as she walked away, called over her shoulder to, 'be sure to say 'hullo' to my Aunt Jeanie for her'.

I realized by then we were never going to be friends, but all the same, I watched her get back into her station wagon and circle the cemetery drive and just as suddenly I was alone again. Me, by myself. I knew I should be getting back to the reunion. I'd been gone for quite a while by now and could feel my cell phone vibrating inside my purse. I certainly didn't want to worry anyone. This was never my intention.

But before I took off, I decided to go back to Ari's grave one last time - just me. I hadn't liked Margo and didn't feel good about her being the sole ambassador of all things Ari. And I likely wouldn't be back to Nebraska for quite a while, if ever. As it was, it had been over twenty years since my last visit. ***This*** time around I was approaching him myself, ***my*** way. Besides, I wanted to thank him for the love he had given to my grandmother -- for giving her her only real happiness, because I knew it had been.

I walked back to his plot and kneeled down next to his grave. I began by telling him that I believed we may have met many years earlier in the Lincoln General Hospital, when I had carelessly walked right into him and ruined his beautiful bouquet of violets. I told him how sorry I was for any suffering he had endured while he was sick and how disappointed I was for him that he and my grandmother never got their shot in life -- because it really did sound like they made a good team. I couldn't think of anything else, so was reluctantly pulling myself up when, inexplicably, I laid back down, right over his grave!

"Oh, why, Ari, *WHY?"* I cried. "Why couldn't you and my grandmother have made it? I realize I, literally, would not be here, blubbering like a romantic fool if you had, in fact, gotten your shot, but still, I wish you had!" And then I whispered, "I believe in your love. I *still* do - despite everything".

And I swear to you, hand to God, some force or wind urged me to that spot a moment longer, and in spite of the heat I was suddenly *covered* in goose bumps as this 'something' compelled me to turn myself around and lay upon an old man's grave. With my gaze facing upwards, I saw it then; I saw it ALL:

I saw the wind move the clouds, as if to part a theatre curtain - the curtains themselves were the goldest gold, nearly too bright to behold - and I saw the ***bluest*** *blue sky you could ever imagine, bluer than my son's large eyes when he was a toddler. And I saw a light so brilliant beaming a sort of pathway to something beyond the clouds and the sky itself. I saw a long white table filled with colorful flowers, yet these flowers were no ordinary flowers; they were* ***dancing*** *and* ***swaying.*** *They seemed to be beckoning me. The atmosphere was littered with violets, their petals lush and purple, swirling about, and a large group of very merry people gathered all around. And no, it wasn't the relatives at my family's reunion, and it wasn't the heat causing me to have some sort of strange delirium. I saw a bride - Hadley - and a groom - Ari - and they were sitting there together with their heads bent toward each other and he was whispering something, for her ears only, and she was laughing. And it sounded like the most beautiful, lyrical melody that hummed inside my ears in perfect pitch. Hadley was lovely and she was thin and there was no longer an angry scar over* *her left eye. She had long shiny hair with violets woven throughout, and handsome Ari looked so proudly at her, fingering her waves and caressing her neck. Next to them was Grandpa Perry - only he was young and UNspectacled - and he had his arm casually draped over the shoulder of a gorgeous redhead, two fishing poles crisscrossed behind their chairs. Lucille was there with a headful of Shirley Temple-like curls, and she was flanked on either side by two men: one appeared tall and gangly, the other seasoned, debonair. She had the undivided attention of both of them and it was more than enough. At last. I saw Papa Ismay, and he was singing - he was wearing a red and white straw hat like the rest of his quartet - only he was also playing a harmonica intermittently between their tune. His fingers were whole and they were nimble and the twinkle in his eye appeared to me like a brilliant shooting star, beaming down from the sky now just for me - and me alone. And I saw great Grandma Bertha, only she was young as well, and trim and... smiling. Bertha was smiling and she was happy, and she was speaking to me, telling me everything would be alright... 'aaawwlll riiightt nowow'... and I just loved the sound of her voice. It was so soothing, as becoming to her as her smile.*

And then I saw the best sight of them all: I saw Buddy! She looked younger than my daughter, no more than twelve or thirteen, and she wore a crown of vivid roses on her head, and she was playing the flute. Her head was bobbing back and forth to her papa's melody, she was like the pied piper and she was summoning everyone up from the long bridal table to dance with her while she led them all. She led them then in a whimsical little dance that had a hop and a skip and two claps to the side. They joined her, even the menfolk, even Herbert - ESPECIALLY Herbert - in a hop and a skip and two claps to the side. She led them toward a vibrant orange Model-A roadster that was similarly adorned with flowers, as well as white streamers; there were shiny gold bells on the ends of them, shining like the chrome on the roadster's spoke wheels. And she was motioning Ari and her sister inside this darling automobile, while she herself was climbing into its rumble seat, and they were leaving the party... they were beginning to drive away and Buddy turned back to wave at them all, these party guests, and... finally... at me - her would-have-been and now will-always-be great niece - and she was blowing me kisses, and I saw there was a sign at the back of the rumble seat and Buddy turned it and it said "Eternally Harry", the sign was swinging back and forth, BACK and FORTH, as a rocker would. As a rocking chair would if someone was sitting in it and abruptly - or finally - got up in search of something more.

Something better.

Eternally...

'Harry'

And there you have the story of my paternal grandmother, Hadley Palmer Wallace... Hough. It is *real,* it is *magical*; it gives me goose bumps still. I hope it leaves you better than it found you, truly I do.

Photography by Derek Jason

Epilogue

A Few Words to the Audience...

Dear Gentle Reader,

I have always dreamed of writing a novel, the kind of tale I wish *I* could read. One which appeals to both young and old, women and men, exquisitely written - though easy to read - with characters that inhabit you while simultaneously coaxing you to think about your own life and what you want out of it. A story that makes you laugh out loud, *cry* and gives you goose bumps. Something that doesn't take too much of your time -- but just might stay with you for a lifetime.

And I have had a true love of words for as long as I can remember. Whether it's a word search, crossword puzzle or scrambler at the back of a children's menu, I delight in playing with words. When I was growing up my father, whose own vocabulary is extensive, would use a word at Dinner, such as 'pugnacious' and then refuse to tell us its meaning; rather insist we leave the table, grab a dictionary and look it up for ourselves. Naturally I never forgot its meaning -- and in fact used it on a playground bully the following school day.

I majored in English Literature in college - so obviously I have done my share of reading - and while I generally have always loved a good book, I think I was really there more for the *words.* When I went to lecture, I would listen very keenly to my professors' dialogues, eager to jot down a new word or two I could adopt as my own. Now I have Google!

Many years later I fell in love with, and then stumbled into teaching, a form of hatha yoga. Because of circumstances that were quite by 'accident', I had no formal training and as such, I was forced to learn how to be an instructor on the fly. What I quickly discovered was how important it was for me to use my words *selectively, compellingly,* in order to teach the most efficient and inspiring ninety-minute sessions possible - that is, to tell the best story.

When I teach a yoga class I also use music to its greatest effect and am extremely fussy about my playlists, and I devised a similar technique to assist myself in the writing process: I'd choose a contemporary upbeat song, such as "La La La" by Naughty Boy with Sam Smith and then listen to something quieter, more soulful, like "Youth" by Daughter, just to be sure a scene I was constructing worked with both moods. I wanted my novel to have a timeless feel despite its being mainly a period piece. (In fact, you may want to re-read the final page of OFF HER ROCKER while playing "Youth" in the background, and I highly recommend Sam Smith's acoustic version of "Latch" for the love scene; if this book is ever turned into a film, I will insist upon its use for Hadley and Ari's night of passion).

I want to share with you here that I am a survivor of one of the rarest forms of pancreatic tumors, (the same kind of tumor Steve Jobs had; coincidentally, I taught hot yoga on several occasions at Apple), and throughout my health scare and lengthy convalescence I had a lot of time on my hands, but not much energy. Books became some of my best friends and partners in healing. The odds of surviving a neuroendocrine tumor to the pancreas are sobering - worse than surviving an airplane crash. After this brush with death, I've tried to never take my life for granted and writing a book absolutely went to the top of my bucket list.

So when I thought I had conceived a hauntingly beautiful, layered story, I sat on a stool, lotus-style, at the desk in my den nearly every day for six months writing... and writing. When I wasn't writing, I was *thinking* about writing. Too often I'd be in the shower and have to dash, dripping wet, across our house to jot something down before it was lost to me, or gotten into bed anxious for a good night's sleep only to find the characters swirling over my head, summoning me back up to play with them. Many times the bills were paid late: there was no way I was getting up from something *this* much fun just to go off to the Post Office for some stamps. I virtually lived in one pair of black sweats: my husband bought me a lounging outfit for my last Birthday and the pants of it now have holes throughout and are frayed at the ends; I've literally worn them out while writing.

Hadley, Ari and Perry have become a part of me; they are as real to me as the fingers of my own hand. Now that I have finished my novel I am going to miss each of them - terribly. I hope you enjoyed OFF HER ROCKER as much as I enjoyed writing it because it was the most fun I have *ever* had on my own. The experience felt very similar to reading a fantastic book, where you simultaneously can't wait to find what happens, yet never want it to come to an end. I hope you found the themes of devastation, mental anguish, moral dilemma and true love resonating: my version of "To Kill a Mockingbird" meets "Splendor in the Grass" with shades of "Stairway to Heaven". I hope I left you by the very last word utterly satisfied - yet *panting* for more. And I thank you most humbly for your time. I have no doubt it is precious.

Oh! I recently purchased a soft black jumpsuit; perhaps it is time to sit down and begin writing novel number two.

Truly,

Diane

Acknowledgements

Writing my first novel, OFF HER ROCKER, has been *such* a labor of love - but in no way was it a solo effort. I simply must acknowledge the tremendous support and uncanny contributions of the following special people:

To my late grandmother, Frances Dorothy Palmer Collman, you are the inspiration behind this tale. Hadley is not quite you, not quite me, but somehow, some way, a spiritual amalgam of the two of us and I thank you for allowing me to take you on this journey. I love and miss you still and have not a shadow of a doubt you are beautiful once more.

To my brilliant father, Dr. James Paddock Collman, I am indebted to you for giving me a love of big words and being so strident about our use of correct grammar. I appreciate the personal details you were willing to entrust to me, particularly on our long, hilly jogs... I hope I made you proud.

To my darling mother, Patricia Tincher Collman, you were a wealth of information for all things Liberty and it was pure joy to interview you. Your fondness for your small town childhood shone through in our chats and I know you sorely miss the way things used to be. What evolved is, hopefully, an opportunity to revisit the past as well as my personal love letter to you.

To my favorite aunts, Betty Jean Thomas and the late Thelma Tincher, I *had* to include you both. Aunt Jeanie, you provided 'Winsdee' nights, vivid tornadoes, Clay Collier and Phil Coburn. Thank-you for your constant humor and for treating this endeavor so reverently. My angel, Aunt Thelma, there was no sweeter, gentler soul. I love, love, LOVED you. Just think: you finally got to be a mom!

To my sisters, Carolyn Collman and Victoria Collman Brown, Thank-you for encouraging my creativity. Vicki, as the oldest sister, I have always looked up to you, my ultimate role model of motherhood and decency. Carolyn, our baby, when we were little girls you were my first audience; as women, the first one I told my story to. Both of you are my forever friends. And to Pamela Collman, I know you loved Grandma best... you were right about that.

To my early readers, Brenda Abdilla, Sheryl Axline, L. Mercedes Hughes Brennan, Vicki Burnett, David Clark, Cynthia Cook, Bambi Larson, Abby Ross & Carole Skinner: Thank-you for your precious time and enthusiasm. Merce, the suggestions you offered absolutely enhanced my story. After more than thirty years of friendship and artistic inspiration, this became our first collaboration; may there be more. Cynthia, any gal who stays up until 3:00 in the morning on her anniversary trip to read something I have written is my best friend for life! And Bambi, thanks not just for reading my first draft so carefully, but for practicing at Yoga Fort nearly every week - and even more - for always inquiring 'if there might be room for you'.

To my students at Los Gatos Yoga Source 2006 – 2012, Thank-you for being the most considerate, appreciative and *captive* audience. You helped me learn to use my words carefully - lovingly - which lent itself so beautifully to the writing process. Guiding your practice remains my favorite job, ever. Don't tell the boss but: I should have been paying *you*!

To my skilled doctors, Oncologist Jeffrey Norton and Hematologist James Zehnder, Thank-you for saving my life in 2008. Dr. Norton, you were my cowboy and hero who rode in on his big horse, kicked up a lot of dust and rescued this damsel in distress. Dr. Zehnder, you are the consummate professional and a true gentleman: discreet, debonair, *kind*. From the moment I met you, you have *always* listened to me; I'm so glad you did. I know I truly beat the odds to be here and want you to know I am grateful to you and the phenomenal staff at Stanford Hospital 2008 – 2009 for each and every extra day. A shout-out to Dr. Mike Rosenthal, my personal friend and all-time coolest adult, for stepping in when the going got tough, and for his impeccable bedside manner.

To our accountant of many years now, Ed Benoe, Thank-you for helping me understand just what it is accountants *do.* I am sure my Grandpa Perry would have liked you. Charlie and I certainly do.

To Nate Divine from Chase Bank, teller extraordinaire, Thank-you for all the 'fun' money you gave me and particularly for the 1935 one dollar bill you sacrificed, which I kept with me throughout the writing process, and was a wonderful link to the past, as well as my good luck token.

To our children, my babies, Taylor Matthew and Jensen Nicole Skinner, you helped too. Tay, you ran a lot of errands for me so that I could keep writing, kept me nourished in Cheese House sandwiches and properly sugared up on See's dark bordeaux. Jeni, you were one of my two most devoted readers, not to mention the sweet touch of Buddy. You will always be 'at the top of prettiness' to me. Both of you are my pride and joy and your mama wanted to give you something you can keep forever.

And to Charles Madison Skinner, my soul mate and partner in life: you are the embodiment of sexy, irresistible Ari, yet you rooted for good and decent Perry - *of course.* You are a tireless champion of all things Diane and have thoroughly ruined me for anyone else. The stories I could tell of your astonishing, endearing gestures would fill up several books and this first one would never, ever, have come to fruition without your steadfast belief in me. What a friend I have in you!